DOORS OPEN ON THE LEFT

AN OPEN DOORS NOVELLA

VINNI GEORGE

Doors Open on the Left

Copyright ©2021 by Vinni George

All rights reserved. No part of this book may be reproduced or transmitted in any form or by any means, electronic or mechanical, including photocopying, recording, or by any information storage and retrieval system without the written permission of the copyright owner and where permitted by law.

Reviewers may quote brief passages in a review.

Cover Design: Cate Ashwood Designs

Editing: Jennifer Smith, LesCourt Author Services

Proofreading: Lori Parks, LesCourt Author Services

First Edition

November 2021

This is a work of fiction. Names, characters, places, and incidents are either the product of the author's imagination or are used fictitiously. Any resemblance to actual persons living or dead, business establishments, events, or locales is entirely coincidental. All person(s) depicted on the cover are model(s) used for illustrative purposes only.

ABOUT THIS BOOK

Strangers on a train...

Dr. Brooks Bruno has one rule: don't interrupt someone when they are reading. But when a sexy stranger boards his train, he's too intrigued to follow his rule. He's also too smitten to remember to ask for the guy's phone number. But he can't get the stranger's face out of his head.

A missed connection...

Henry Miller has always been a hopeless romantic, so when he meets a gorgeous guy who loves books as much as he does, he's pretty sure he's *the one*. Unfortunately, Henry is too caught up in their literary banter to ask the important questions...like his stranger's name.

A second chance at love...

In a city as big as Chicago, finding each other again will be nearly impossible, but sometimes fate intervenes in mysterious ways.

Doors Open on the Left is a book #2.5 in the Open Doors world featuring a jaded English literature professor, a bookstore owner who loves romance novels, a human shop cat, and a secret identity. It can be read as a standalone but is best enjoyed after Revolving Door *and before* A Foot in the Door.

1

BROOKS

JUNE

"DAMN IT!" I hitched my messenger bag higher on my shoulder and stuffed my phone into my pocket. The clatter, screech, and spark of the approaching "L" train meant I was cutting it way too close. Missing this train would mean having to battle the touristy baseball crowd as they made their way to the bars around Wrigley before the afternoon's home game. Why people wanted to sit outside to watch a sport that was, in my opinion, far better enjoyed from the air-conditioned comfort of home, I'd never know. I liked occasionally going to Wrigley for the overpriced beer and hot dogs, but that was about it. On a ninety-degree day with eighty-five percent humidity, hard pass.

The train was rounding the last curve before my stop, and I was still a block away. Kicking it into high gear, I sprinted the remaining distance—I really needed to get back to the gym—and pulled my transit card from my pocket as I ran.

Shockingly, the light on the console turned green after the first pass of my card in front of the reader—an early June miracle. I bolted through the turnstile and took the stairs two at a time. I was way too out of shape for this shit, especially when it felt like I was drinking the air through a tiny cocktail straw more than breathing it. Chicago in the summertime was humidity and tourists, neither of which I particularly liked, and the fact that it was already so hot didn't bode well for the former. Jury was still out on this year's tourists. I hit the platform and rushed into the first train car I could reach as the doors slid closed behind me, nearly clipping my bag as I pulled it around my body.

The barely functioning AC fought against the heat from outside and the bodies already filling the train. It was a losing battle. I fell into a side-facing seat as I tried to catch my breath and not focus on the sweat dripping down my back beneath my shirt. Why had I decided teaching a summer session was a good idea? Oh, wait. I hadn't. I'd been pressed into what amounted to indentured servitude by Dr. Butler, department chair and total douchebag. *The tenure committee will look more favorably on your resume if they see you are dedicated to teaching, Dr. Bruno.* I wanted tenure. Well, my dad, lifelong academic and currently tenured law professor at Northwestern, wanted it for me. Academia was the family business after all. My mom had been an archaeology professor before she died in a freak accident during a dig in Jordan when I was five. She had died for academia, a fact my dad hadn't let me forget when he was pushing me to get my doctorate.

As the days got hotter, I would only begin to loathe the trek from my apartment to the MacMillan University campus more. The twenty-seven minutes I spent on the train were even worse on Mondays, Wednesdays, and Fridays when the end of the trip meant standing in front of a room of bored undergraduates while trying to make them care about American Literature from the late nineteenth century. Spoiler alert: also a losing battle.

Instead of using the commute time to review my notes on *Daisy Miller* for class, I pulled out my phone to jot down a few bits of dialogue that were running through my head. I'd started writing during grad school as a way to procrastinate, and I'd published my first novel a few years ago after my friend Stacey, who worked as a literary agent, had read it and insisted on pitching it. I wasn't hugely prolific, but I had a solid fan base, and my books sold well. I was supposed to be noodling a new series, though nothing had officially come of it yet. Much to my dismay, it seemed I was experiencing a bit of writer's block, even though my characters were still infinitely more exciting than my students. Not for the first time, I wondered if there was a way to turn my writing career into my only career.

Argyle is next. In the direction of travel, doors open on the left at Argyle.

After more than a decade, the mechanical train voice was part of the background soundtrack of my time in the city. Part of the consistent hum of over two million people moving in the same space. There was an odd comfort in it.

My fingers flew across my phone screen as I banged out the dialogue for the scene that would hopefully turn itself into a full novel. Though I wasn't really that hopeful. I'd been struggling to write since I'd finished my dissertation application. My theory was that the hell of putting together my CV had sucked the creative energy right out of my soul. It had been nearly impossible to get into a groove, and the harder I pushed, the worse my writer's block seemed to get. The fact that I had an idea I thought I could work with was reassuring. For the moment.

The train slowed, then the doors opened letting in a blast of moist summer air. I adjusted in my seat, unsticking my pants from the backs of my legs, and my phone buzzed in my damp palm.

Beckett: How about Thai?

Beckett James, a friend and fellow professor at MacMillan University who taught super complicated statistics classes, and I had a standing Friday lunch date. It was too early to be thinking about lunch, but Beckett liked a plan.

Me: We did Thai last week…
Beckett: Indian?
Me: Meh…
Beckett: Brooks… I am not eating at Lou Malnati's again.
It's too hot for pizza!

It was never too hot for pizza. I started to type my reply, but a flash of movement caught my eye. I looked up and watched as a man fell into the seat across from me. His face was flushed from the heat but stunning, if you liked nerdy chic, which I did. I *so* did. He had windswept golden-brown curls that were just a smidge too long, dark thick-rimmed glasses that were maybe just this side of out of style, a smattering of freckles across the bridge of his nose and over his high cheekbones, and green eyes that… had just caught me staring. *Shit.*

While I'd been drooling over the bespectacled guy across the aisle, Beckett had continued to text, but I hadn't even felt my phone vibrating.

Beckett: Brooks?
Beckett: ???
Beckett: Fine, I'll eat the fucking pizza, but I swear you will regret this choice.

I smiled. Silence had always been the fastest way to wear Beckett down.

Me: You're lucky I'm in the mood for Chinese.
Beckett: Oh thank god! Spring Garden at 1:30?
Me: See you then! You're buying!

I switched back to the dialogue I'd been writing, grateful I finally had a few words flowing after months of nothing, and chanced a glance at the cute nerd across the aisle. He had a book in his hands and looked totally enthralled, the nail of one of his thumbs held between his teeth as his eyes moved across the page. I knew that feeling. The enthralling power of a good story was the only reason I'd made it through four years of undergrad and seven years of graduate study. Writing stories I hoped captured my readers in the same way was the only thing keeping me from losing it on a daily basis.

I glanced quickly at the book's cover, then did a double take. A copy of that cover hung over my desk at home.

Nerdy Chic was reading one of *my* books.

I had never seen one in the wild before. I mean, I'd seen them on bookstore shelves, but I'd never actually seen someone *reading* one. Maybe I'd seen someone reading a copy on their Kindle, but I didn't know because it was impossible to tell what someone was reading on an e-reader unless you were close enough to read over their shoulder. Which I tried never to do.

It was kind of weird but also completely awesome to see someone actually reading a real paperback, and an added bonus to see they were so into one of my stories. He smiled around the nail he still had clamped between his teeth, and I wondered what part he was on. I was dying to know.

"What are you reading?" I asked. Interrupting someone while they were deep in a book was something I typically considered one of the most abhorrent breaches of etiquette, but the words had slipped out without conscious thought—cute guy reading a printed copy of my book and all.

He looked up and saw me watching him. "Did you say something?"

I gestured to the book. "I asked what you were reading."

"Oh. *Kryptonite*," he said glancing at the cover.

"Do you like it?" *Please say yes*, I silently begged. If he said he hated it, it would be a rejection from which I'd never recover. Okay, that was probably a little melodramatic, but fear of public rejection and criticism was reason number four hundred eighty-five why I refused to do appearances or signings despite constant nagging from Stacey, my friend slash publicist slash agent. I couldn't explain it, but knowing what this guy thought of my work meant something to me.

He put his finger between the pages to mark his place and looked up to meet my eyes. God, his eyes were fucking beautiful. "Yes."

With one word, my heart soared. "Tell me about it."

"Do you really want to know or are you just trying to hit on me?" It was a legit question. I already knew what the book was about, so technically I didn't need to know plot details, and yes, I was *trying* to hit on him.

"I really want to know. You were smiling as you were reading, so it has to be good."

His face relaxed, and he sighed a little wistfully. "It's great, actually. This is the third book in the series, and the books are all noir-type retellings of classic superhero stories. It's a really interesting approach. I've read everything this author has written." He took a deep breath, looked down at the book in his hand, then looked back up at me, a light blush staining his cheeks like maybe he realized he'd said most of that without a pause.

It was my turn to smile. "Really? Have they written a lot?" I couldn't stop myself from fishing.

"R.W. Cook has only been writing for a few years, but he has two series out. This one and another one that is six books. His first series is all classics from the perspective of the antagonist. Those are really interesting because they again take a contemporary suspense approach to novels I honestly thought were pretty boring when I was in high school and college."

"Oh?"

"Yeah. My favorite book in that series is *A*. It's basically *The Scarlet Letter* but from Chillingworth's perspective. He's a forensic scientist whose wife, the Hester Prynne character, leaves him, but he really doesn't care until he gets a weird letter from Hester's adult daughter claiming she thinks her mother was murdered and asking him to help her investigate."

Wow, this guy really did know my stuff. His interest in my writing was an unexpected ego boost. I wanted to tell him I'd written the book he was holding, but I wasn't sure how to bring it up. Before I could ask another question or tell him I was the author of the book he was reading, he continued talking.

"It's really cool how the author turns the villains into antiheroes. I've always been a sucker for a bad good guy."

I couldn't hold in my laugh and several other occupants in the train car turned to look in our direction. "Who's your favorite?"

"Classically or in Cook's antihero series?" he asked, and my heart rate kicked up. I wasn't sure how I knew it, but this guy was practically perfect for me. Last semester, the senior seminar I'd taught had been all about canonical antiheroes.

"Classically." I leaned forward placing my elbows on my knees and getting as close to my train companion as I could, desperately awaiting his answer.

"Easy. Jay Gatsby." That was one hundred percent the correct answer. Nerdy Chic was proving to be more and more perfect with each passing second. I schooled my reaction so as not to show too much excitement about this development. Stimulating literary debate turned me on like little else, and I was already half-hard. Or maybe that was because my brain had somehow conjured a picture of my train companion reading my book naked, lounging on a divan à la Rose in *Titanic*.

"Gatsby. Interesting choice. Why?"

He looked me squarely in the eye, and a shiver raced down my spine. Then he said, "It all comes down to motive. He was motivated by love for Daisy, and all his choices, right or wrong, revolved around finding a way to get to or keep her. But Gatsby doesn't get his happily ever after, and I always thought that was a little sad." He looked down at his lap where he held my book, his finger still marking his place. "I'm a little bit of a hopeless romantic."

"Interesting. Though you could argue despite—"

This is Fullerton. In the direction of travel, doors open on the left at Fullerton, the automated train voice interrupted.

Fuck. "This is my stop," I said, standing and grabbing for the handrail. The movement caused my bicep to flex, and my train companion's attention traveled from my face to where my arm bunched against the confines of my short-sleeved dress shirt as I tried to keep my balance on the slowing train. He swallowed hard.

"Oh…" he said with a hint of regret in his voice.

"It was great talking with you." I turned, keeping one hand on the handrail and putting the train car doors to my back so I could maintain eye contact for a few more seconds.

The doors whooshed open, and I felt the wall of heat from the Chicago summer at my back. I tried to stall, wanting just another second to chat, but the other departing commuters jostled me out of the way, and I was forced out onto the platform. As I was shuffled forward, I swore I heard him say, "You too." I turned as soon as I was out the doors. As the train pulled away, I tried to catch one more glimpse of the bespectacled hottie. That was also the moment I started mentally kicking myself for not getting his name or number. Apparently, having a doctorate didn't mean I was intelligent.

D minus for the day, Dr. Bruno. Not even an E for effort.

2

HENRY

"GOOD MORNING, Mrs. Matthews! I put a new pillow on your chair, and the coffee in the pot is fresh."

"Thank you, Henry. And good morning to you too, sugar," Mrs. Matthews said, rummaging inside her huge turquoise fake-alligator bag. Apparently unable to find what she was looking for, she set the bag on the floor and bent over to rummage more deeply. Mrs. Matthews was maybe four foot ten, and her turquoise bag was so big she could probably fit inside it. As she searched the depths of the tote, her whole head and most of her shoulders were swallowed up. I was starting to wonder if she could breathe in there when she emerged, triumphantly holding her leopard-print glasses case. "Do you have the new Janet Evanovich yet?" she asked as she slid her fuchsia readers out of the case and perched the glasses on her nose. I rolled my eyes. We'd had this discussion every day for the last three weeks, and while I loved her, I was over it.

"Not yet," I said through just slightly gritted teeth. "It doesn't come out until November."

"Oh, that's right! I have to set a reminder for that one." She rummaged in her big blue bag again and came up with a large smartphone in a rhinestoned case. "What was the date again?"

"The twelfth," I said with a forced smile. I had shown her how to add events to her phone's calendar the previous week, and if she remembered how to do it today, I might have to reconsider believing in a higher power.

"Okay, got it." I highly doubted that, but I wasn't going to argue. "I'm off to hit the Harlequins. Call me if you need me!" She slung her massive bag over her shoulder, teetering a little under the weight, gave me a finger wave, and puttered through the archway into the larger-than-strictly-necessary romance section. I breathed a small sigh of relief that I didn't have to explain her smartphone to her yet again and settled in behind my desk. I had a mountain of paperwork to get through and new release orders to place. It was going to be a busy day. I'd been working for only a few minutes when I heard the telltale scraping sound of wooden legs on a hardwood floor that was Mrs. Matthews moving a chair around, muttering about "more light." I rolled my eyes and reminded myself this was what I'd always wanted out of life.

Mrs. Matthews treated my bookstore, Tiny Tales, like it was a library. In the five years I'd owned the store, she'd only missed coming in a handful of days, and to my recollection, she'd never bought anything. But she was sort of awesome in a quirky way and kind of like the wacky grandma I'd never had. I treated her a little like I would treat a shop cat. I made sure she had coffee and snacks, and I kept the bathroom clean and stocked with Charmin because it was her favorite brand of toilet paper. In return, she read my romance novels and was careful to never crack the spines. Occasionally, she would provide words of wisdom.

Nestled between two giant buildings in Wicker Park, my bookstore resided in a converted row house that had somehow escaped the renovation boom in the area. A family foundation owned the building, and I once got a rather unprofessional letter telling me they had no plans to sell to "corporate assholes." I was fine with that, especially since they hadn't raised my rent by even a penny in five years.

The store had retail space on the first two floors with storage on the third. The first floor was made up of my desk slash office area slash cash wrap, a small Chicago writers and Chicago history section in the front room by the door, and the romance section in the room to the rear. The second floor had more general fiction—classics, sci-fi, fantasy, and mystery—and some biographies and cookbooks. The third floor was general storage at the back with extra toilet paper and paper towels, replacement shelving, and back stock, but it also had an amazing nook with a cantilevered leaded-glass window that stuck out over the sidewalk below. It would make an awesome office or writing space. It didn't make sense for my desk to be upstairs when I was my only full-time employee, but I hoped to one day make the nook usable. I had secondhand armchairs and comfy cushions tucked into crannies all over the first and second floors, and the walls were painted in warm neutrals. The hardwood floors had seen better days, but I'd covered the worst of the worn spots with soft area rugs and tried not to wince too much when the floors creaked in the winter. My shop was my favorite place on the planet. My inventory was made up of everything I loved to read, from the classics to science fiction and romance, especially romance, and quirky literature-themed gifts and tchotchkes I couldn't resist. And Mrs. Matthews, human shop cat extraordinaire, was generally well behaved around customers.

Before I could place the orders I needed, I had to do a quick inventory, so I walked through straightening shelves and making notes on a Post-it about what I needed to fill. "Doing okay?" I asked as I walked into the romance room.

Mrs. Matthews was settled into her favorite armchair, which she'd moved closer to the window and positioned just so. A coffee cup was perched on the wide arm of the chair, and she had a

Harlequin in her hand. She gave me a thumbs-up, and I moved around her to finish checking stock.

As I settled behind my desk, my mind kept wandering to my conversation with the auburn-haired stranger on the train earlier. It seemed I was doomed to be distracted by him all day. My meeting with the handsome stranger had been a stupid ten-minute interaction, but I couldn't shake thoughts of the man. Visions of his intense hazel eyes as he'd asked me about my favorite antihero kept staring at me from my mind's eye, and I kept scolding myself for not getting his number or at least his name. It was probably something mysterious like Matthias or Fabian. Maybe I read too many romances. I sighed and tried to refocus on my bookkeeping. The numbers weren't great. I pushed back from my desk, knocking over a cup of pens and pencils and the novel I'd been reading on the train.

"Shit." The clattering drew Mrs. Matthews to the front room.

"What's up, buttercup?" She took me in as I knelt to pick up the mess. "You seem a little stressed."

I didn't want to burden her with my problems, but I remembered she'd once told me she'd helped her late husband start a very successful business. She couldn't work her smartphone, but maybe she could help me figure out how to get more people in the door.

"I'm not really happy with the way things are going. I need to get more people in the shop, but I don't have any idea how to do it."

Mrs. Matthews rubbed her hands in glee. "Hold that thought, sugar." She spun on her Keds and trotted back to the romance room. I heard shifting and shuffling and knew she was neck deep in her bag again. "Here we go." She pulled up a chair.

"Why don't you make yourself comfortable." I rolled my eyes.

"I am quite comfy, thanks." She flipped open the pink glitter notebook she held, flipped to a page that had a lot of writing on it, and slid her readers down from the top of her head. "I have a list."

"A list? A list of what?"

Mrs. Matthews gave me a look over her glasses that told me I was clearly a moron. "A list of ideas for what you could do to liven this place up a bit. Get some butts in the seats as it were."

"When were you planning on sharing these ideas with me?"

She huffed. "You never asked. And it wasn't my place." I shook my head. Mrs. Matthews had an opinion on everything, and she'd never kept herself from sharing before.

"Uh-huh."

"You're ready now."

"Uh-huh."

"Do you want to hear my ideas or not?"

I wasn't sure I was ready, but… "Okay, proceed."

Mrs. Matthews cleared her throat. "First, you need a float in the Pride parade."

My jaw hit the floor. "I can't afford—"

She held up her hand, cutting me off before I could finish voicing the protest. "I know you can't, but what about that librarian and booksellers group you belong to?"

Huh. That was actually an interesting point. The LGBTQ Booksellers and Librarians Association had been tossing the idea of sponsoring a float around for a while, but no one had pulled the trigger. "It might be too late for this year. It's already the beginning of June."

"Nonsense. People drop out all the time. When's your next meeting?"

I glanced at my watch to check the date. "Tomorrow."

"Good. Bring it up. One of the people in your group has to know someone who can pull some strings if registration is closed."

She had a point there. Last I heard, Eric's partner was on the Pride planning committee.

"Okay. I like that idea. What else have you got?"

Mrs. Matthews ran her finger down the list then tapped on one of the entries. "You need to host a Drag Queen Story Hour. Everyone loves it."

I didn't hate that idea either, and I had a decent-sized children's section that wasn't getting as much use as it should. Eric did drag. Maybe he could help get a story hour started too.

"That's actually a really good idea. I'm a little mad you've never mentioned these things before."

She reached across the table and patted my hand. "Like I said, you weren't ready."

"All right, all right. Any other genius plans?"

"Of course. I think you need to get some local authors in for signings."

"Like who?"

Mrs. Matthews wiggled in her chair and sat up straighter. "I'm so glad you asked." She picked up the book I'd been reading and flipped to the end. "R.W. Cook lives in Chicago where he spends way too much time enjoying Chicago-style pizza and hot dogs and not enough time taking advantage of the lakefront biking and running trails. He does not have any pets, but he enjoys dog sitting for his neighbor's dachshund, and he would consider a pet of his own one day, though it would probably be a fish. When he's not writing, he can be found cheering for local Chicago sports teams, but he'll never say which Chicago baseball team he prefers." She huffed. "Bet it's the Cubs. I wonder if he's cute. Why is there no picture? Janet Evanovich always puts a picture."

I raised an eyebrow in her direction. "I thought you were helping me bring in business, not helping me find a date."

She smiled. "Why can't it be both? Anyhoo, you see what I mean? You love this guy, and he lives here in the city. I have a whole list of authors."

"I can't just email them and ask if they want to come sign books at my tiny bookstore."

Mrs. Matthews pursed her lips and tapped a finger against them for a second. "Okay, then put out an ad and let them come to you. Maybe this guy"—she smacked the book she'd set on my desk—"won't answer it, but I bet you'll get some interest. Once you have a calendar going, you can advertise at the local universities. I bet a bunch of professors would make their students attend if you did readings or Q&A sessions with the signings."

My heart rate sped up. What I wouldn't give to meet R.W. Cook. He'd never been to a signing as far as I knew, and his website never mentioned live appearances. But what if he came to my shop? That would be the highlight of my career. I started a mental checklist of all the places I could put out ads. Mrs. Matthews was right. I might not get someone as big as R.W. Cook, but signings and readings were a great way to build interest. I actually felt like an idiot for not thinking of it myself. I'd just hoped people would magically find my shop. Maybe I read too many fairy tales.

"I love this idea. Thank you."

She stood from her seat. "No problem. You let me know when you're ready for more ideas." She winked, and I turned back to my computer to start putting together an ad.

3

BROOKS

ANOTHER FRIDAY, another lunch date with Beckett. I was seated across from him in a red folding chair at one of the few tables at Kameya, a hip, if tiny, sushi restaurant not far from campus, rehashing my meeting with Nerdy Chic on the train. The guy had been on my mind a lot over the last month. I didn't know why I couldn't shake him from my memory. It had been ten minutes of my life, but it felt somehow significant.

"I wish people besides serial killers still used Craigslist," I said as I used my chopsticks to pick up a piece of hamachi. "I could post a missed connection and then he would see it and we could fall in love and have fantastic discussions about books and make beautiful little babies with tiny plastic-framed glasses."

Beckett grabbed my hand. I had apparently been gesturing wildly with my chopsticks, and he must have been afraid of getting hit in the face with flying fish. "First of all, that's weirdly romantic for you. Second, biology is still in play here, so there would need to be others involved for you to have beautiful babies, though yes, I am sure they would be lovely. And third, you've really got to let this go."

"I know."

"Do you, though? It's been a month."

I picked up another piece of fish. "Yes. I know. It's just… I can't get this guy out of my head. What if he was the one, and I let him slip through my fingers?"

"Remind me why we're friends. I didn't sign up for this flowery bullshit, but I suppose it's my own fault for spilling coffee on someone from the English department. This is cosmic retribution, isn't it?"

Beckett and I had met when we were both getting coffee at the campus coffee shop. He'd turned quickly after picking up his order and dumped his iced latte all over me. I'd asked him out. We'd gone on one date and decided we would be better as friends. That had been four years ago, and as of yet, we'd been unable to get rid of each other.

I shrugged. "Probably."

"You know, you could try this new app I consulted on."

"Eh, the apps aren't my thing." One too many dick pics for me.

But Beckett was not to be dissuaded. He picked up his phone from where it had been sitting on the table between us and furiously tapped away, his top lip trapped between his teeth, a sign of his intense concentration as he searched for the app.

"Here. It's called DIBS." He turned his phone around to show me the screen, and after I'd acknowledged the icon, he set his phone on the table again. "There is a section for missed connections and a marketplace for selling stuff. It's basically a Chicago-specific, non-creepy Craigslist app. A buddy of mine from grad school is the head of data analytics for them, and I did some initial consulting for him when they were first starting out. You aren't the only person in the city who is trying to find their stranger on the train. The app generates all sorts of interesting data."

"Only you would use the word *data* when referring to a hookup app."

Beckett gave me "the glare." He usually reserved the look for particularly stubborn data sets and grad students he was mentoring, but if necessary, he would turn the look on me.

"Don't knock metrics. Data is very important, Dr. Bruno. Just because you deal in fiction and fantasy doesn't mean the rest of us don't prefer cold hard facts. Also, it's not technically a hookup app."

Beckett's phone had been buzzing on the table as we'd been talking, and he picked it up, going quiet for a minute, his lip pinned between his teeth again. I took the time to once again mentally kick my own ass for focusing more on the promise of literary banter and less on the practical logistics of seeing my train guy again and getting his name. With his name, I could have at least tried to find him on social media. Okay, that was a lie. I was terrible at social media stalking. I would have had Beckett do it.

"Everything okay?" I asked when Beckett set his phone down again.

"Yeah. Sam is just having a meltdown."

"Sam? Your cute blond friend with the glasses?"

"Wow, you really do have a type, don't you?" I shrugged as Beckett continued. "Yes, that's Sam. A guy we went to college with is starting at Sam's company next week, and he's flailing."

"What's the big deal? Does Sam not like the guy or something?"

Beckett laughed. "That is the exact opposite of the problem. Sam liked the guy a little too much in college. It's a long story, but let's just say Sam hates change, and his company is going through a bunch of changes right now. Adding Max Martino to the mix is guaranteed to send him off the deep end."

"Got it." I picked up a piece of California roll and shoved it into my mouth.

"Also, nice try at deflection, but I know your tricks," Beckett said as he flipped his phone over on the table so he couldn't see the incoming messages. "I think you should give the app a try."

I rolled my eyes. "Fine. I'll consider it."

"While we're on the subject and you seem potentially more amenable to my ideas than usual, can I show you something else?"

"You're going to do it whether I say yes or no, so just show me."

"Fair." Beckett picked up his phone again and clicked around, then handed it to me.

"People use the *Reader* for more than cheap apartment listings?"

"Apparently." He gestured at the phone. "Read."

The screen showed an ad looking for Chicago-area authors who would be interested in doing readings or signings at a bookstore called Tiny Tales in Wicker Park. There was an email address and a phone number people could use to ask questions or get additional details.

"I don't do public appearances. I try to keep a low profile, and I don't want the university to find out. You've met some of my colleagues," I said, trying to pass the phone back to Beckett.

Beckett winced. "Lots of people in your department publish, though. I don't understand what the big deal is."

"They publish academic work."

"That one guy." Beckett snapped his fingers trying to recall the name he was looking for. "Big bushy beard, wears suspenders all the time. What's his name?"

I laughed. "Dr. Winters?"

Beckett slapped the table "Yes, him. He publishes fiction. You dragged me to that big reception last year."

"He writes historical fiction. It's hardly romantic suspense and mystery with gay undertones."

Beckett scoffed. "Publishing is publishing, right?"

I shook my head. "It's really not. Dr. Butler would have a

field day if he found out what I write. Maybe after I get tenure. My dad has already been giving me shit about how he's not hearing good things about my application. He'd have a total fit if he found out I was still writing after I told him it was just a hobby."

"I've said it before. This whole thing is stupid. You and I both know you don't really want to be a professor for the rest of your life. What if writing could be your full-time gig?"

It was something I'd been considering more and more often. "I don't know. My dad—"

"Brooks, you're thirty-three. Does your dad really get a say in what you do?"

Son, academia is the family business. But it was feeling less and less like the right fit for me.

"I was at this bookstore during Pride. My friend Nash is a librarian, and they hosted a Drag Queen Story Hour thing. It's not usually my scene, and there were way too many kids, but I was intrigued, so I went."

"I have questions, but I'll hold them for now. What does Drag Queen Story Hour have to do with me doing a signing?"

"It could be a two birds, one stone kind of thing."

I set my chopsticks down and sat back, crossing my arms over my chest. "Explain."

"The place was cute. Like the name suggests, it's small. Like tiny. Only sixty to seventy people could fit in the whole place. It could be a nice way for you to dip your toe into the public appearances pool, especially if you want to make writing a full-time thing. You've said Stacey wants you to go to signings. This could be a nice start."

One of my eyebrows quirked. "And?"

"And I met the owner. Trust me when I tell you he is exactly your type."

"You just said you wanted me to try your new app."

Beckett waved my words away. "There's nothing wrong with

trying both. You could reach out to Henry, that's the owner's name, and put up a profile on the app."

I didn't really want to do either, but if I didn't give Beckett a glimmer of hope, I'd never hear the end of it. "We'll see."

———

A WEEK LATER, I was sitting in the smaller of the two English department conference rooms, listening to Dr. Butler drone on about the end of the first summer term during our one and only summer faculty meeting, when my phone vibrated in my pocket. I was seated far enough out of Dr. Butler's sight line that I could check the notification without attracting too much attention. As department chair, he was a member of the tenure committee, and as much as he bored me, I didn't want to risk incurring his wrath. He was a tiny guy who insisted on wearing tweed even in the dog days of summer, and a man who could wear tweed in July was not a man I wanted to anger.

Beckett: Have you contacted the guy from the bookstore yet?

I chanced a glance at Dr. Butler, who was talking about curving and his personal disdain for the practice, before I responded.

Me: Umm…
Beckett: I'm taking that as a no! You need to reach out to him. What's the worst that can happen? You don't like what he has to say, and you decide not to do a signing.
Me: Fine.
Beckett: Good. BCC me so I know you've done it. Have you posted on the app yet?
Me: Umm…

Beckett: Brooks!
Me: I told you I'd think about it.
Beckett: You've been thinking about it for a week. Do it now and send me a screenshot, or I'll do it for you. You said he had a great ass, right? I'll lead with that.
Me: I hate you.
Beckett: *winky face emoji*

A look at the clock told me I had to endure Dr. Butler for twenty more minutes before I could escape to find something for lunch. I figured I could use the time wisely to write the stupid email. I logged into my author email account, composed what I thought was a short, sweet, and to-the-point message, and hit Send. Dr. Butler moved on to the next topic while I downloaded Beckett's stupid app and thought about what I wanted to say. Even a month later, train guy's face was still fresh in my mind, and he'd been playing a starring role in my latest fantasy reel— heated literary debate followed by heated… *ahem*. I was skeptical my mystery man would ever see the post, but at least Beckett would get off my ass about it. I put together something that was probably too generic and would likely yield a whole bunch of responses that weren't my guy and texted Beckett a screenshot like the dutiful best friend I was.

Beckett: There's no picture. You have to include a picture.
Me: He's never going to see this. I'm not posting a picture. And you said it wasn't a hookup app.
Beckett: It's not. How is he going to know it's you without a picture?
Me: He can message me, and I'll ask him a question only he'd know the answer to.
Beckett: It would be easier to just post a pic.

Dr. Butler looked my way, and I stashed my phone under my

thigh. When his attention swung toward a group of grad students who were teaching the summer sessions of the intro composition classes, I pulled it out again. I was as bad as my students.

Beckett: I saw your email. Nicely done.
Me: Are you happy now?
Beckett: Very. Keep me posted.
Me: You'll nag me until I do.
Beckett: Truth.

Maybe Beckett was right. God, he'd be insufferable if he ever found out I thought so. Maybe I should consider a signing. I loved the idea of making writing my full-time career. Sure, it would disappoint my dad, but he'd get over it, and it would be better than being miserable for the rest of my life.

My phone buzzed again, and the notification said I had a new email. It was a response from the owner of Tiny Tales providing the extra information I'd asked for. The message said he wanted to keep things small since his shop wasn't huge, and he hoped for a fifteen-to-twenty-minute reading with a Q&A session and signing to follow. The more I read, the more interested I became, but it would still be a big risk, and I wasn't sure I was ready to put myself out there. I glanced at the clock and mentally ran through the rest of my schedule for the week. Maybe I needed to check out Tiny Tales on my own as Dr. Brooks Bruno, English professor, before I made any decisions about doing a signing as R.W. Cook.

4

———

HENRY

I dropped the box of books I was carrying and hustled into the romance section. "Mrs. Matthews! Are you okay?" She looked fine and was perched in her usual chair by the window. She had her phone clutched in her hand and her readers on her nose. I nodded toward the phone. "Is everything all right?"

She waved me over. "I downloaded this new app, and I like to read the personal ads. Reminds me of my favorite section of the newspaper back in the day. Anyway, I was scrolling through the recent posts, and I think this one might be about you."

"What? What are you talking about?" I circled the chair and tried to read over her shoulder.

"Do you remember where your man got off the train?"

As if I could forget. I'd only staked out the train station two dozen times since that day and tried at least once a week to retrace the route I'd taken that morning to see if I could run into him again. So far, my efforts had yielded nothing. I didn't know what else to do to try to find him. "Fullerton."

"Here. Read this." She thrust her phone at me, and I looked down at the enlarged type, scanning the words. "Out loud."

I huffed then read. "Dear Hopeless Romantic, I saw you on the southbound red line. You were reading a book and humored me when I interrupted. I got off at Fullerton, but you've stayed on my mind. Let's meet for coffee and to talk books. P.S. Jay Gatsby is my favorite antihero too."

"So is he talking about you?"

"Honestly, I dunno. What if this is like his pickup technique or something? It's been a month. If he was looking for me, why didn't he post sooner?"

Mrs. Matthews rolled her eyes and slid her readers to the end of her nose, looking over them at me. "Who are you, and what have you done with my hopelessly romantic Henry?"

"What do you mean?" I pleaded.

"I mean, this"—she made a broad, sweeping gesture with her arm—"is the kind of thing you live for, angel. You go call or text or email or Snapbook or Facechat that man right now!"

I snorted; it couldn't be helped. "Snapchat. Facebook."

"Does it really matter at the moment? No! The point is you get in touch with this man however you have to!" She maneuvered herself behind me and started pushing me back toward my desk, and for a second, I was distracted by the strength in her tiny frame. "He sounds like a keeper! And after you snare him with that gorgeous butt of yours, you ask him if he knows Janet Evanovich."

I knew my freckles were doing nothing to hide my blush. "Mrs. Matthews." I groaned as I gave her a look that told her I wasn't amused. Though if I were being honest, I knew my butt was something special. Squats really did pay off.

"I'm just saying. Now scoot! I'll be listening."

"I know you will, which is why I'm going to respond via the app." God bless the twenty-first century.

She turned to head back to her chair and her Harlequin, but I heard her mutter, "Dammit. You're no fun," as she went.

Waiting for a response to my response to the missed connection ad sucked. It was better when I'd thought it was just a missed opportunity neither of us had taken, but now thinking tall, smart, and handsome was rethinking his choice to post the ad was making me a little anxious.

I was also distracted by the email I'd received from R.W. Cook after I'd posted my ad looking for local authors. He'd seen it and had asked for additional information. It had been a banner day for communication from elusive mystery men, but the waiting for their responses was literally going to kill me.

I paced through the front room and straightened the Chicago history books… again.

"Henry, my darling dear," Mrs. Matthews said from her chintz perch, "this is an old building. While the floors seem sturdy, they are not meant to withstand that kind of pacing."

"Why hasn't he responded yet?" I snapped back, unwilling to concede her point.

"Who?"

"Either of them. Ad guy or R.W. Cook."

"Because it's only been a half an hour. Forty-five minutes at the most."

I sighed dramatically. "True love waits for no man, Mrs. Matthews!"

"Wait. Now which one are you talking about?"

"Either."

"I can't believe you hesitated to reply to the ad."

I sent a glare her way she couldn't see.

"I can feel you glaring at me," she said with an imperious chuckle that echoed through the shop.

I sighed again and went back to my desk. I had accomplished the sum total of nothing so far and needed to make headway on a few things before Drag Queen Story Hour later. My buddy Eric had jumped at the chance to start a story hour when I'd brought it up. He said his drag persona, Miriam Webster, was made for it. In fact, he'd planned our whole Pride float around the theme. That had been another huge success. We'd had a steady stream of new business since, and I owed Mrs. Matthews big time for her suggestions.

I was just about to pull up QuickBooks to see if I could finish some bookkeeping I'd started earlier when my phone vibrated in my pocket. I glanced at the notification to see it was a message from the DIBS app. I bobbled my phone in my hands, caught it, and then opened the app to read the message.

ProfGatz24: Hopeless Romantic?
RmanceRdr: I hope so…
ProfGatz24: Hmmm… how to figure this out?
ProfGatz24: Do you wear glasses?

Yeah, me and half the city of Chicago.

RmanceRdr: Yes…
ProfGatz24: What do they look like?
RmanceRdr: Dark, plastic frames… not super stylish.
ProfGatz24: It could be you… What book were you reading when we met?
RmanceRdr: *Kryptonite* by R.W. Cook

If this was my train guy, he could be my kryptonite.

ProfGatz24: It is you!
RmanceRdr: It is me!

My heart was beating double time. My mystery guy had found me, or I'd found him. Either way, this was the kind of thing epic romances were built on. So now what? Before I could think of a reply, my phone buzzed again.

ProfGatz24: Can we meet for coffee?

RmanceRdr: Yes. I'd really like that. When?

Now? Say now! I mentally begged. I would kick Mrs. Matthews out and meet this guy wherever he wanted. Speaking of Mrs. Matthews… I looked up and shrieked, nearly toppling backward out of my chair. She was bent over with her elbows on my desk and chin held in her hands, coyly batting her eyelashes at me. Evidently, the old lady was also a ninja. I was going to have to get her a bell.

"Did he respond, Henry? I didn't hear you pacing, so I came to check on you. Don't worry, I've only been staring at you for the last few minutes."

I rolled my eyes at her and reminded myself she was almost a paying customer. "Yes, he responded. Go back to your book, and I'll fill you in when I have details to share."

"That smile says you already have details, sugar snap!" she said with a wink and nod toward my phone.

"Go! Or I'm buying Angel Soft for the bathroom." I made a shooing motion toward the other room.

"You wouldn't dare!"

"Try me!"

She harrumphed. "I'm going, I'm going. I really should just start going to Bingo."

I should be so lucky. I turned my attention back to my phone to see more messages from ProfGatz24.

ProfGatz24: Tonight?
ProfGatz24: Too soon?
ProfGatz24: Yep, too soon…

Shit. I couldn't meet up with him tonight. I had story hour. I glanced at the clock. It was too late to cancel.

RmanceRdr: NO! Not too soon. I just have a work thing I can't miss tonight. Rain check?
ProfGatz24: Definitely!
ProfGatz24: My name is Brooks by the way.
RmanceRdr: I'm Henry.
ProfGatz24: Henry. That suits you.
ProfGatz24: Damn. I have to go, but can we chat later?
RmanceRdr: Definitely!

———

Phone clutched to my chest, I stood and did a happy dance. How was this my life?

———

"HAVE A GREAT NIGHT," I said to two moms and their two little boys, the last of the attendees from that evening's Drag Queen Story Hour. I wasn't trying to push them out per se, but I was dying to message Brooks again.

"Phew! I don't know about you, but I'm pooped, sugar," Mrs. Matthews said as she pulled the trash can overflowing with scraps of colored paper and foam from the story hour craft to the front room.

"Me too. Why don't you head out? I can take care of the rest of cleanup."

"Are you sure? There really isn't much left."

"I'm sure. I've got it."

She smiled. "How did the shop do tonight?"

"They almost cleaned me out. I've already made a list of things I need to reorder before next week, and one of the little guys who just left demanded I stock more *Pete the Cat* books, so I've added those to the list too."

Mrs. Matthews patted my arm. "I'm so happy for you."

I bent and kissed her cheek. "It's all because of you. This was all your idea."

She blushed but waved my comment away and strode to my desk to grab her big turquoise bag from where she'd stashed it. "See you tomorrow, sugar."

"I'll be here." I waited until she was out the door and the bells on the door handle had stopped ringing before I headed back into the children's section to finish picking up and resetting the room. I hadn't been at it for too long before I heard the bells on the door jingle again.

"What did you forget?" I yelled over my shoulder as I stacked tiny plastic chairs.

"Hello?" The deep voice was somehow familiar, but it definitely wasn't Mrs. Matthews's.

"Give me one second. I'll be right there." Stacking the last chair, I surveyed the room, cataloging the last things I needed to put to rights. I straightened some shelves as I went. "So sorry. We had a children's event here earlier. Is there something I can hel—"

The rest of the words got caught in my throat as the gorgeous hazel eyes I'd been dreaming about for the past month met mine. Standing in my shop on a random Tuesday night was my stranger from the train. He was just as perfect as I remembered with his tousled auburn waves, strong jaw covered in the barest hint of an auburn beard, and broad shoulders. My eyes wandered from the top of his head to his feet in a slow once-over that made my heart pick up speed. His eyes raked over me in the same way, and I felt his gaze like a caress lighting up my skin and no doubt making me blush. I wasn't sure what he was doing there, but he seemed just as surprised to see me as I was to see him.

"Henry?" he asked.

I nodded. "Brooks?" How had he found me? I replayed our text conversation. Nope, I definitely hadn't told him where I worked. Did this mean he would have found me even without the app? If so, it must be fate, kismet, destiny. I locked my knees so I wouldn't swoon.

Brooks smiled, and the most adorable laugh lines appeared

next to his eyes. He wasn't much older than me if at all, but those lines told me he spent a lot of time smiling. I loved that.

He held out his hand, and I unstuck my feet from the floor so I could cross to where he was standing.

When my palm connected with his, a shock skittered up my arm leaving heat and a pleasant buzzing sensation in its wake. During our time on the train, I'd thought we had chemistry—I'd felt it arcing between us as we'd spoken—but now I knew it. One look at Brooks's face, his eyes wide and his lips parted in a silent *O*, told me he'd felt it too.

"How did you find me… I mean, how did you find Tiny Tales?"

Brooks squeezed my hand, sending another charge through me, then released it. "A friend of mine was here for an event during Pride. He suggested I come check it out."

"I'm so glad you did." I felt my cheeks heat and realized how lame that had sounded. I needed a minute to get my head on straight. "Feel free to browse. I'm just going to, uh, head over there and finish cleaning up." I really wanted to fling myself at him, but there was excited and then there was desperate. I was trying to avoid the latter.

Brooks's eyebrows arched. "Um, yeah, sure."

"Chicago writers and history up here. Romance, if you're so inclined, is through the arch. Kids and young adult over there"—I pointed over my shoulder—"and general fiction, the classics, mysteries, etcetera, and general nonfiction and cookbooks are on the second floor. Stairs are in the romance room."

"You've got quite the collection." Brooks looked around and leaned forward to peer through the arch to find the stairs.

"I stock what I like to read."

His eyebrows hit his hairline again. "Surely you've not read all of these."

I laughed. "Oh, heavens no. I just stock my favorite genres. You'll notice the nonfiction section is heavy on memoir and only a few others. I hate self-help, so if you're looking for that, you won't find it here."

Brooks laughed, and the sound settled somewhere low in my gut. I wanted to wrap myself in it and hold it close to my heart always. And that was my cue to leave before I said something that sappy out loud.

"I'm just gonna…" I pointed a thumb over my shoulder.

"Okay. I'll just…" Brooks pointed the other direction, and we both backed away, our eyes still locked, until I bumped into a shelf and had to turn to steady it and myself. When he was out of sight, I did a little happy dance. This was unbelievable. Unreal. After a month of stalking train routes and trying to time my routine just right, Brooks and I had found each other twice on the same day. That kind of coincidence didn't just happen if a thing wasn't meant to be. My heart swooped and fluttered in my chest. Maybe this was the beginning of the epic love story I'd always wanted.

Rein it in, Henry. What if that day on the train was a fluke? But no. Fate wouldn't be cruel enough to place Brooks in my path again if that were true. I shrugged off the thought and got back to work, still a little shocked at the day's turn of events but really excited. The effervescent fizz in my bloodstream was heady and a little addicting.

As I stacked the rest of the chairs, wiped down the two low kiddie tables, and ran a quick Swiffer over the floor to pick up as much glitter and tiny scraps of paper as possible, I heard Brooks moving around upstairs. I tried to place what section he was in, but I couldn't quite tell.

Once I had the Swiffer put away, I went to find him. I had decided while I was cleaning that I was going to ask him out for coffee, even though we technically had already put a pin in that idea earlier, but I was determined to see my plan through to setting a date and time. I wouldn't let Brooks get away again. It took a lot for me to put myself out there. Over the last five years,

I'd been doing it less and less, using the shop as a reason to avoid dating. I hadn't been lying when I'd told Brooks I was a hopeless romantic that day on the train. Unfortunately, love wasn't often found on hookup apps, unless you were only looking for love that lasted one night, and I wasn't. I wanted the big romance-novel-type love. I wanted the rakish pirate who would plunder and pillage my body and the depths of my soul. Maybe Brooks could be my pirate. He could totally be a cover model if he unbuttoned a few extra buttons on his shirt.

And I really needed to stop letting Mrs. Matthews recommend my reading material. She'd been on a pirate kick lately, and it was clearly bleeding into my subconscious.

Brooks was in the mystery and romantic suspense section. He was looking at the shelf of R.W. Cook books I had on the endcap. The floor creaked as I approached, and he looked up.

"You really are a fan, huh?" he said when I got closer.

"I really, really am." Brooks had a funny look on his face, and I couldn't place the emotion. It almost looked like surprise, but that didn't track. I'd been reading an R.W. Cook book on the train, and I'd confessed to being a fan then. He obviously remembered that. "I'm not the only one. These are actually some of my best sellers. I just restocked them this morning."

"Really?" His surprise turned to shock, and he mumbled something under his breath that I didn't catch.

"Did you know the author lives in the city?"

Brooks looked away. "He does?"

I picked up one of the copies of *Kryptonite* off the shelf and flipped to the author bio at the end. "Yep. See?" I handed Brooks the book, and he took it but didn't look down at the page.

"Interesting."

"There's no picture, so I have no clue what he looks like. There isn't a photo on his website either. I wonder if I've ever passed him while walking on the lakefront or ridden next to him on the train. That would be so weird, right?"

Brooks still hadn't looked up at me. "Yeah, weird," he said, his voice low.

"He actually responded to an ad I posted looking for authors to do readings and signings here at the shop. I sent him more details, but I haven't heard back yet. It would be so amazing if he actually agreed to do it, but I'm not holding my breath."

Brooks had gone a little pale, and his face was contorted like he'd sucked on a lemon. He made a weird noise in his throat. I took the book from his hands and put it back on the shelf. Once he was no longer holding the novel, some of his color returned. Weird.

"Um, I was wondering…" I said at the same time he said, "Can I ask you something?"

Brooks laughed. "You go first."

I rubbed a hand over the back of my neck. "Can we schedule that coffee date now?"

Brooks's answering smile crinkled the skin at the corners of his eyes again, and I wanted to reach out and trace the lines. "I was going to ask you the same thing."

"I'd love to. When are you free?"

"I'd say now, but it's late, and I don't want to seem too eager. How about tomorrow?" Brooks beamed at me, and my heart turned over in my chest.

"That sounds perfect."

5

———

BROOKS

It was the perfect name for the guy I'd met on the train. He looked like a Henry.

As I paced around my apartment, I couldn't figure out why I was so nervous. Henry and I had similar interests, and I knew we wouldn't lack for conversation. I just hoped I'd be able to unearth some sort of flirting skill so I could turn this date into something more. I felt like I had no game. Did people even say that anymore? Fuck. I was proving my own point. I'd never been good at initiating casual hookups. Not that I wanted this to be casual, because I didn't. God, I was a mess. Thirty-three and past my romantic prime. At least I could blame the mid-July weather for any sweating I was doing. I had already changed my shirt twice. This was a second chance, and I didn't want to blow it.

Henry lived in Uptown, which wasn't far from where I lived in Edgewater. We'd agreed to meet at one of my favorite coffee shops, which was near my apartment, so to kill time, I texted Beckett and filled him in on the latest developments.

Me: So we are on for coffee tonight…

Beckett: I can't do coffee tonight. Hot date with a guy from my gym.
Me: No, asshole. Not me and you. Me and the guy from the train.
Beckett: What?! How?!? I feel like I missed something.
Me: He responded to my post on the app. And he's your bookstore guy. Henry.
Beckett: Henry?
Beckett: Wait… Henry from Tiny Tales is your train guy?
Me: Yep.

My phone rang, and I tapped the screen to answer it.

"You're shitting me, right?"

I rolled my eyes. "Hi, Beck."

"Tell me what happened. How did you figure out Henry was the guy?"

"It was a bizarre coincidence, really. He messaged me back on the app, and we started chatting. I asked him out for coffee, but he said he had a work thing—"

"I've told you, there are no coincidences, only statistical probabilities. Though I have to admit you finding your guy from the train had pretty low odds in a city this size without knowing exactly where he lived and only being able to triangulate the data to stops along the red line between Granville and Argyle."

"You ran the math?"

"It's cute you think I wouldn't. Anyway, how did you end up at Tiny Tales?"

Standing in front of my mirror, I gave myself a critical once-over. It wasn't perfect, but it would have to do. "I went by to check it out last night."

"Why? Are you considering doing the signing?"

"I'm thinking about it."

"Brooks! That's awesome. You need to. The shop is cute, right?"

"Very. Anyway, we're meeting at Metropolis soon."

"I don't know why you like that place." We'd had this debate more than once. I liked my coffee to taste like coffee. Beckett liked Starbucks.

"The coffee is good, and it's close to my house."

"Whatever. Let me know how it goes. Also, I told you Henry was totally your type."

"I'm flipping you off right now."

"Rude. Did Henry flip out when you told him you were R.W. Cook? I know you said he was a fan."

My stomach pitched. This was the part of the whole thing I still hadn't reconciled. I was afraid if I told Henry I was one of his favorite authors, he would only want to date me for that reason. Sure, we'd had great chemistry and a lot in common on the train, and last night at his shop I'd gotten the distinct impression he was trying to avoid climbing me like a tree—which I would have been all for—but I didn't want to complicate things just yet by revealing my secret identity. More than that, I didn't want to disappoint him and doom our relationship if I decided I didn't want to do a signing. "Um, I didn't tell him who I was."

"Brooks!"

"I know, I know. But I like him, and I want him to like me for me."

"You need to tell him. You *need* to."

"I will… just not today."

"When this bites you in the ass, can I say I told you so? I don't need to run the numbers to know the odds on that."

"Fuck you. I'm hanging up now."

I stabbed the button to end the call and shoved my phone into my pocket. The constant buzzing against my leg told me Beckett was still telling me off via text.

The coffee shop wasn't far from where I lived, so I set out that way about twenty minutes before we were scheduled to meet. I didn't want to get there too early because waiting in the coffee shop would be far worse than waiting at home. At home I could freak out, in public not so much. I still wasn't exactly sure how I'd gone from pining over train guy to finding him and going on a date with him in less than twenty-four hours, but I wasn't fool enough to question it.

The quiet stroll through my neighborhood was the perfect time to collect my thoughts. I waved to Stanley, my neighbor Mr. Oliveria's slightly overweight dachshund, who was out in the yard next door, which sent him waddling to the fence and following me to the end of the block.

The breeze blowing off the lake was doing nothing to cool the air, and the humidity was still oppressive, but I somehow felt refreshed in a way I hadn't since the spring. The closer I got to Metropolis, the less nervous I felt. When I was a block away, I noticed a man with brown curls standing outside, and I caught a glint of sunlight off the lenses of thick-rimmed glasses. As I approached, Henry turned, and as I got closer, I felt my body react. He was gorgeous and so much my type I couldn't control my reaction. I willed myself to think of the Cubs' most recent box score against the Cardinals to keep any unwanted erections at bay —it had been way too long since I'd been on a date—and greeted Henry.

"Hi, Henry."

He held out his hand like he had last night at the bookstore. I shook it, the same surge of heat I'd felt yesterday pulsing up my arm. His hand was soft and dry despite the humidity, and I couldn't resist awkwardly pulling him into a hug. He smelled like lemons and new books. It might be my favorite smell in the world.

As we stepped apart, I noticed the green in his eyes wasn't a pure green but a combination of green, gold, and blue. We hadn't been close enough for me to see the swirl of colors last night, but it was stunning, and I found myself staring again. I cleared my throat and looked away. "Should we go in before we melt in the heat?"

"Yes, let's."

I held the door and let Henry pass in front of me. As he did, I tried in vain not to check out his ass, but I totally did. He was wearing tight gray khaki shorts that were cupping that ass in all the right ways, and I needed to pull out the Cubs' box score again before my mind wandered to places it shouldn't on a first date. There was no use denying it. I wanted him. I'd wanted him that day on the train, and last night in his shop, and this morning when I'd jerked off in the shower. Honestly, I'd wanted him every day for the last month. I wasn't normally like this, but it was almost like Henry had put me under some sort of spell. The heat that had pulsed through my blood during our handshake and hug was proof.

Metropolis roasted their own coffee, and the smell of roasting beans had been pungent even outside, but now it felt a little like we were standing inside a bag of coffee beans. Usually I loved the bitter smell, but I was suddenly self-conscious about my choice of date location.

As though he'd read my mind, Henry said, "I love coffee shops that roast their own beans. There aren't too many local places that do that anymore."

"Me too," I said, relaxing a little.

We walked up to the counter. I ordered an iced latte, and Henry ordered an iced mocha. Since it was still summer, the college kids who normally filled the coffee shop were blessedly absent, and we were able to grab one of the couches near the windows after retrieving our drinks.

"So," we both said at the same time, then laughed.

"I'm sorry," I said, looking at the buttons on his tight button-down instead of his face. "I don't know if you've noticed, but I'm really terrible at the small-talk thing. Plus, I find you really attractive… which was probably a really awkward thing to say. I blame too many years spent in the library, not enough time socializing."

Henry blushed and laughed a little, but it wasn't at my expense. "I understand. I spend the majority of my time talking to a septuagenarian and sometimes forget how to talk to people who aren't just a little bit strange."

It was my turn to laugh, and I appreciated that he was trying to make me feel more comfortable. "Tell me about the strange septuagenarian."

"Her name is Mrs. Matthews. I've known her for five years. She comes into the shop every single day and reads the romances, but she never buys a damn thing. She carries a huge purse that I swear could be a body bag, and sometimes when she's looking for something in the bottom, I'm afraid she's going to fall in, and I won't be able to find her. She's like a zany great aunt I'm luckily not related to, but I think she's really just lonely. I know she's a widow, and she told me once she doesn't like to hang out with people her own age because they tend to die on her. Recently, she actually gave me some really good ideas to improve traffic in the shop, and as much as I complain, I'd miss her if she wasn't there," Henry said with fondness.

Add *kind to old ladies* to the list of pros Henry had going for him.

"She sounds kind of great."

"Yeah, she really is."

"How did you end up owning a bookstore?"

As Henry started to talk, his face lit up, and I could tell he loved his shop and his work. I didn't have that kind of passion. Maybe for writing, but I'd never really talked about it to people who hadn't been there since the beginning. My dad didn't approve since he fell firmly into the "academic writing is the only kind of writing" camp, so I didn't talk to him about it either. I could probably, at a stretch, get him on board if I wrote memoir, but he'd never think genre fiction was worthy of my time. Even

Beckett got a sort of manic gleam in his eye when he spoke about his latest project or a tricky statistical analysis project. The best that could be said for me was that I didn't run screaming from the building at the end of every workday. Henry's passion for his shop was something to behold, and if possible, the light in his eyes made him even more beautiful. I wanted that kind of passion in my life, and it made me wonder what Henry would look like when he came. Which was, again, a completely inappropriate first date thought.

"It was my dream. I've always loved to read, and I always wanted to own a bookstore. I was lucky enough to know someone who knows the owner of the property and they connected us. I opened five years ago. I have an online store too, so that helps, and I work with some of the local universities to carry things the campus bookstores have trouble sourcing. I just started a biweekly Drag Queen Story Hour, which brings in lots of family traffic. But I'm really in it for the books. It's a little embarrassing since I'm a thirty-one-year-old guy, but I love romance novels. You've seen the romance section at the shop. I love genre fiction, so, as you saw, I carry a lot of that too. Some people probably think I should move on to more 'mature' reading, but I like what I like, and it makes me happy," Henry said. "What about you? What do you do?"

Henry touched my knee where I'd folded my leg under me, and I felt the heat from his hand move through my body. The electricity that burned through my veins was more potent than the heat of the Chicago summer, and it took me a second to remember what we'd been talking about. I covered his hand with mine and threaded our fingers together. When I looked up, I was happy to see another faint pink blush under the freckles across Henry's cheeks. He smiled encouragingly.

"I'm an English professor at MacMillan University," I said, and Henry's eyebrows rose. He was no doubt thinking about our brief Gatsby discussion on the train. "I'm only an adjunct, so I don't make a ton of money. I finished my PhD three years ago and have been at MacMillan since. There's supposed to be a tenure track position opening up this year. I've applied, but it's a waiting game. I have a committee meeting in September."

I stopped myself from confessing I was R.W. Cook. I really liked him, and given the way he'd fanboyed a little on the train and again at his bookstore, I knew telling him would change things between us. Besides, I still hadn't returned his most recent email asking if I wanted to pick a date to do a reading and signing. The weight of every word in that email settled heavily on my shoulders, and I shifted in my seat. But who even knew if there would be an R.W. Cook for much longer. Despite the few lines of dialogue I'd written—on an idea I'd thought had promise but had really gone nowhere—the day I'd met Henry, I'd been completely blocked since I'd turned in my tenure portfolio. I hadn't even set foot in my office in over a week. What would Henry say if he found out one of his favorite authors was already washed up and out of ideas? No. There was no way I could tell him.

"Do you like teaching?" Henry asked.

The million-dollar question. "Sometimes. I feel like my students have gotten spoiled, though. I know it sounds silly since I'm not that much older than some of them, but they want to know everything right now. They don't want to work for it. They don't want to debate. They just want the 'right' answer." I sighed and moved my hand from his to run it through my hair. Henry moved his hand farther up my thigh and the corresponding pulse of heat through my body caused me to shift as blood rushed south.

"I'll debate with you," Henry said looking at me through his lashes, a flirty smile on his face.

I hoped he would, but I also wanted to do more than talk, though the conversation so far had been nice. I trailed my fingers up his arm and felt him shudder under my touch. Hmm, maybe I had more game than I'd thought. "I think I'd like us to do more than debate."

Henry smiled, then licked his lower lip and bit it with his teeth. My eyes followed the movement with rapt attention, and my body leaned forward without me telling it to, pulled farther into Henry's orbit. Henry's lips against mine had been all I'd been able to think about since that day on the train, and I wanted to kiss him more than I wanted to figure out my life.

The time between our first meeting and this moment had given me time to work up fantasies where he took the starring role, which might account for why it felt like we'd known each other longer than we had. I wasn't sure I believed in soul mates, and I was sure Beckett would have something cutting to say about the statistical likelihood of there being a single person for any individual in the world if I ever brought it up, but there was something about the man sitting next to me that made my heart kick up and scream *Mine*. It was a completely foreign sensation for me and as terrifying as it was thrilling.

It felt like a critical moment between us, like there was an invitation hanging in the air, and if I didn't take it, I'd always wonder what would have happened if I had. I moved my hand from Henry's shoulder to the back of his neck and gently but firmly pulled him closer. He gasped and then relaxed into the hold and let me bring his face closer to mine until our noses touched and then our lips brushed. The first kiss was tentative and sweet, a gentle sweep of lips against lips. I pulled back and opened my eyes to find Henry's still closed behind his glasses. God, he was cute as hell, even when I couldn't see his eyes. I studied him for a moment too long, and his eyes popped open.

"Are you waiting for an invitation to do that again?" he asked a little snarkily, and I thought in that moment that he might have been made for me. A slightly sarcastic, nerdy-chic bookstore owner who liked the smell of roasting coffee beans and read my books. He might just be perfect.

Instead of answering, I leaned in and brought our mouths together again. My nose was full of his lemon-and-book scent, my hands were full of his firm, soft skin, and I wanted my mouth full of his taste. I teased the seam of his lips with my tongue, and he opened for me with a soft sigh. I explored his mouth with mine, and he returned the exploration in kind. He tasted like the mocha he'd finished and something deeper and infinitely more complex. We kissed for long moments until the clearing of a throat nearby caused us to shift apart.

As I came back to myself, I remembered we were still in the middle of Metropolis. Our little make-out session had garnered more than a few stares and a silent slow clap from the barista behind the counter, who made eye contact and shot me a thumbs-up before turning back to the customer in front of him. We were lucky our hands hadn't started wandering.

"Shit," Henry whispered, his head still leaning against mine.

I wanted so much more, but I got the feeling it wasn't the right time. I didn't want Henry to think I was only in this for the sex. "I'd invite you back to my place, but I really want an excuse to see you again. Can we do dinner this weekend? I know a great Thai place that isn't far from here."

Henry smiled, and his eyes lit again. "Definitely. Friday?"

"That's perfect." We stood from the couch and tossed our empty drink cups. Once we were on the street, I grabbed Henry's hand and he twined our fingers together. At the train station, I leaned in and gave him another kiss, which ended with Henry backed against the brick wall of the station, my hands in the back pockets of his shorts. The kiss earned a chorus of cheers from a group of teens who were loitering nearby. It was all I could do to pull away and not tow Henry down the street in the opposite direction toward my place.

"See you on Friday, Brooks," Henry said against my lips.

"Friday." After one last kiss, I stepped back, letting our hands stay linked until the last possible second, then walked backward, watching as Henry ducked into the train station.

At the corner, I watched as the train pulled in, and Henry got on. As I turned to walk home, I felt lighter than I had in a long time, and I knew in my heart this was the beginning of something amazing.

6

HENRY

"YOU WERE RIGHT. THAT WAS AMAZING," I said as I pushed my plate away. The Thai place Brooks had suggested was tiny, but the food was some of the best I'd ever had, and I considered myself a little bit of a Thai food connoisseur.

"I'm so glad you liked it." Brooks reached across the table and put his hand over mine.

"I loved it. One day I'm going to go to Thailand. I plan to explore temples and eat my way through the country."

"That sounds amazing. Have you done much traveling?"

"Not at all. The last trip I went on was to Myrtle Beach with my family when I was twelve. I think that's why I have all these grandiose travel plans. I want to see the world. What about you?"

Brooks laughed. "I've been to Canada. Niagara Falls. That's about it. My dad wasn't super interested in traveling after my mom died. I think he blamed her wanderlust for the accident."

He had told me about his family over dinner earlier. My mom and I weren't close, but I knew she was there if I needed her, and if I really felt like I needed a mom hug, she was only five hours away in Carbondale.

"That makes sense." I flipped my hand over and squeezed Brooks's fingers.

The server brought the check, and before I could reach for my wallet, Brooks had his out and was slipping her his credit card.

"Hey! I wanted to get the check," I said.

"This date was my idea, so I'm paying. You plan the next date, and I'll let you pay."

"Deal."

The server brought over the credit card receipt, and Brooks signed it with a flourish. "Are you ready?"

I nodded.

Brooks leaned in and whispered. "Great. Let's get out of here. I'm dying to kiss you again."

God yes. Since our coffee date and kiss on Wednesday, I'd thought of little else. Brooks had been front and center in my daydreams, and I'd felt a little awkward looking him in the eye when we met at the train station before our dinner date, knowing I'd jerked off more than once to thoughts of his hands and mouth all over my body. I was more than ready for more of him.

"Yes, please," I said on a breath, and Brooks's answering smile could have lit up a city block. He slid out of the booth and pulled me to my feet.

Out on the street, he used our interlaced hands to pull me against him, and his lips landed on mine. In that second, I forgot we were on a busy Chicago sidewalk in front of the cutest Thai restaurant in history, and I melted into him. The sounds of the city slipped away until there was only us. I could hear only Brooks's breathing and the sound of my pulse rushing in my ears as my heart tried to divert blood to my brain when it was dead set on heading south.

Brooks rocked his body against mine, and the heat of him was no match for the summer air around us. The screeching of tires and the sound of someone laying on their horn brought us back to reality. Brooks's fingers had somehow tangled in my hair and my hands were clenched in the fabric of his shirt. I stepped back and smoothed the fabric with my palms, which meant I got to run my hands over his chest. Brooks vibrated under my touch.

"I don't mean to be forward, and I know it's only our second date, but I'm just going to throw this out there… I only live a few blocks away. Do you want to come back to my place? I have ice cream," Brooks said, putting a bit more space between us and giving me room to decide what I wanted to do next.

"Lead the way."

The three-block walk to Brooks's apartment passed in a blur of attempted small talk. Blah, blah, blah, "great bakery," blah, blah, blah, "nice neighborhood." But my mind was focused on getting his hands on me again. The fleeting touches at the restaurant and the kisses at the coffee shop and on the sidewalk had been nice, but I was ready for more. I hoped we were on the same page.

When we reached his building—an adorable brownstone—and Brooks unlocked the door, I was more than ready to resume the kissing we'd started earlier. But first, we apparently had to climb the stairs to the third floor. *Sigh*. He finally unlocked his apartment door and held it open so I could step in first. My inner romantic swooned a bit at the chivalry. The last guy who had tried to date me thought chivalry meant making sure the stall door was locked when we rendezvoused in the bathroom at one of the bars on Halsted. I wasn't opposed to quick and dirty, but I liked this much better.

Brooks's space was cozy and perfectly befitting a college professor. From the entryway through an arched doorway, I could see a living room with a large plaid couch peppered with throw pillows. One of the walls was floor-to-ceiling bookshelves and almost every spare inch was filled. There was a worn, overstuffed leather chair in the far corner beneath a floor lamp and next to it was a side table with a potted plant that had seen better days. Down a short hallway in the other direction, I could make out the edges of the kitchen's white cabinets and off the hallway were three doors leading to what I assumed were bedrooms and a bathroom. The art on the walls was eclectic and colorful, and the whole space was lived-in and homey.

"I love your place," I said as I moved into the living room to check out his bookshelves. "These old brownstones have so much character between the arches and the wide moldings. So many little nuances." I slid my hand along a shelf of literary criticism.

Then I felt Brooks behind me. His hand came around my hip, and he bent to nip lightly at my ear.

"Do you really want to talk about architecture right now? Because I will if that's what you want, but I've been dying to get my hands on you since I saw you get off the train before dinner, and that kiss wasn't enough."

I shivered, swallowed hard, and leaned back into Brooks's body. "No. We can discuss architecture another time." Or never. I was fine with never.

Without further invitation, Brooks grabbed my waist, spun me around, and locked his lips to mine again. My hands went to his shoulders, and I kissed him back with equal ferocity. I bit gently at his bottom lip, and his surprised gasp gave me the perfect opportunity to slip my tongue into the warm heat of his willing mouth. As our tongues met, Brooks backed me up against the wall of bookshelves. He nudged my legs apart with one of his and pushed his hips flush against me. His erection brushed against mine, and I moaned as I threw my head back, knocking it into what was probably the shelf of critical theory I'd been looking at earlier.

"Easy," Brooks whispered, nipping and sucking along my neck. One of his hands came up to massage the back of my head where I'd hit it and then stayed tangled in my curls. I moved my hands to Brooks's waistband and tugged at his T-shirt. I moaned again as he found the spot behind my ear that had my knees buckling and goose bumps spreading across my skin.

"You taste so good right here," Brooks murmured against my skin, and I tightened my grip to keep from slipping.

"Need more," I said as Brooks stepped back allowing me better access to pull at his shirt. I slid my hands under the soft fabric and ran my fingers along his stomach, sliding my hands and his shirt up his chest. He stepped away slightly and allowed me to pull the shirt off over his head. He was leanly muscled with gentle definition in his abs and pecs. I appreciated his professor's body and was glad he hadn't been hiding a gym rat under his T-shirt. His pale skin looked rosy in the evening sun filtering in through the living room's picture window.

"You too," Brooks said as his fingers moved to the buttons of my shirt. As he worked them open, I took in his reddish-brown hair, hazel eyes, and angular features. He was lovely. With longer hair and a billowing shirt, he could easily grace the cover of one of Mrs. Matthews's regency pirate novels. All he needed was a little tousling, so I ran my hand through his hair and completed the picture. Brooks was handsome with his hair neatly styled, but with it a little mussed, he was gorgeous. My heart and my cock both twitched a little as I took him in.

Brooks slid my shirt from my shoulders, and as it fell to the floor, I felt his gaze travel from my shoulders to my hips. I wasn't a hairy guy, so all he got was skinny nerd from neck to waist, but Brooks clearly approved as he pulled me closer and brought our mouths together again. I found myself back against the book-shelves as Brooks kissed a path down my neck, over my Adam's apple, and across my shoulder. I reached for his waistband, but he stilled my hands.

"It's my turn," he said.

He continued his exploration, moving his mouth and tongue over my clavicles as his fingers came up to brush, and then stroke, and then lightly pinch my nipples. My cock was hard and starting to ache, and I realized I'd been rocking against Brooks's hip, seeking more friction. Brooks's hands moved to my waistband

and popped the button on my shorts. He cupped me gently and caressed my balls through the material for a moment before finally lowering the zipper and then pushing my shorts and boxer briefs down my legs. My head tipped back to rest against the shelf behind me as Brooks touched my cock for the first time. He stroked the shaft a few times and then traced the vein that ran from base to tip. He thumbed the slit and collected the precum gathering there. His eyes met mine as he brought his thumb to his mouth and sucked it clean. Before I could react with more than a gasp and a hard exhale, Brooks sank to his knees.

"I need another taste." He breathed out as his tongue licked across the slit and then ran along the edge of the head. I panted and was sure I was mumbling and pleading as I watched Brooks tease me. Finally, when I thought he would torture me with tiny licks and strokes of his tongue until I went wild, his lips closed around the head of my cock. I jerked and my hands released the shelf they'd been white-knuckling to tangle in Brooks's hair.

"Please. More," I begged. He responded with extra suction and a flutter of his tongue against the underside of my cock. I shuddered. God, he had a talented mouth. Brooks continued to lavish attention on my cock as I felt his hand reach around to cup my ass. He grabbed a cheek in each hand and squeezed. I moaned my satisfaction and thrust forward into his mouth.

Brooks lifted one of my feet out of my flip-flop and the tangle of my pants and then hoisted my leg over his shoulder. The angle gave him more access to my ass, and while one hand continued to squeeze and massage, the other caressed my crack and teased at my hole. When Brooks pressed gently on the puckered skin, I nearly came.

"Stop. Stop. I want to come with you inside me," I said, drawing a quick breath and trying to reel myself back from the edge.

Brooks smiled and looked up at me from his spot on the floor. "Are you sure? I like this just fine." He bent his head and licked over the crown of my cock again, almost making me forget what we'd been talking about.

"Me too, but yes, I'm sure. I want you inside me." I wanted my hands on Brooks and I wanted to feel us pressed together skin to skin. Normally, I wasn't so eager, but Brooks had me craving him in a way I hadn't craved anyone in a long time.

"Bedroom?"

I nodded and Brooks stood and grabbed my hand. I kicked out of my other flip-flop and left my pants and underwear in a heap on the living room floor. Brooks kicked off his shoes by the door as he led me down the short hallway. He flipped on a bedside lamp, then turned and pushed me back onto the queen-size bed in the middle of his bedroom. I watched as Brooks stripped off his shorts and briefs and fumbled in the bedside table drawer for supplies. He checked the condoms under the light, mumbling something about "expiration dates" and "a long time" and I laughed out loud.

"Sorry," he said. "I should have checked earlier, but I didn't want to be too optimistic."

"Are we good?" I asked.

"We're good."

"Excellent. Get up here."

He tossed the lube and condoms onto the bed and moved to join me. I rolled him to his back and straddled him, then leaned down to kiss him. My glasses slid down my nose and Brooks reached up to remove them. He set them on the table and returned to kissing me. As our tongues dueled again, I rocked my cock against his. Brooks grabbed my ass, squeezing and kneading it in his hands that were surprisingly strong for an academic.

"I've thought about getting my hands on you almost constantly since that first day on the train."

I smiled and rocked against him harder, and before long we were both panting. I found the lube in the folds of the blanket and handed it to Brooks. He popped the cap and slicked up two fingers. The moment felt familiar and comfortable, like we'd done this a hundred times before. There wasn't the normal awkwardness of getting to know someone's body, and the heat, joy, and pleasure that shined in Brooks's eyes undoubtedly mirrored the emotions in mine.

As his first finger tentatively explored my crease, I leaned forward and kissed his neck, giving him better access. His finger traced my rim and then breached my hole, and I let out a little gasp. Brooks moved his finger deeper, and the pressure was wonderful. It had been a while since I'd done this with a partner, and it wasn't the same with toys. Brooks slid his first finger out and added a second. The stretch was more intense, but I'd always liked the feeling. Brooks expertly stretched and massaged my hole until I was writhing and panting on top of him. I couldn't wait to feel his cock inside me.

"Do you want a third?" he asked from below me, and I shook my head. I found the condom, tore it open, and passed it over.

"Suit up, cowboy." Brooks slid the condom on and lubed his gorgeous cock generously. He was well equipped, and I was definitely going to enjoy this.

"If we're doing it this way, I think you're the cowboy in this scenario."

"Shhh," I said placing a finger over Brooks's lips. Joking around during sex was new for me, but I loved it, and it felt like something in my soul clicked into place as I laughed when he bit the finger I had on his mouth.

I levered up and positioned his cock at my entrance before slowly sliding down. I took him in inch by inch, not because I needed to go that slowly but because I wanted to watch the tortured expressions play across Brooks's face. It was just a little bit of payback for the teasing he'd delivered during the blow job earlier. When I was fully seated and my ass rested against his groin, he groaned.

"Please move," he begged, and I was happy to oblige. I set a reasonable pace and Brooks thrust up to meet each of my downward strokes. I shifted forward so every thrust hit me just right, and soon we were both begging for release.

"God, right there. Oh fuck!" I yelled.

"Yes," Brooks panted, his hand coming between us to wrap around my cock. He must have grabbed the lube at some point because his hand was slick as it wrapped around my shaft and worked me in time with our thrusts. I could feel my ass spasming as my orgasm approached head-on.

"Oh! Oh fuck." I gasped as I coated Brooks's fist in my release, my ass clenching around his cock.

"Fuck," Brooks said as he thrust up into me one last time. His muscles went rigid, and I felt his cock swell as he released into the condom.

I lay against Brooks's chest as we recovered, and I thought about how nice it would be to not have to move. I also reflected on how my fantasies of my mystery train man had paled in comparison to the reality. A few moments later, Brooks moved me off him so he could ditch the condom and clean up. There was a door to the right I hadn't noticed that led to the bathroom, and Brooks came back a few seconds later with a warm washcloth and tossed it to me.

"That was amazing. Thank you," I said as I finished with the washcloth, and Brooks chucked it into the hamper. I turned and reached over to the bedside table to grab my glasses, then slid them on.

"It was more than amazing. And I should be thanking you." Brooks was sitting on the bed next to me, still naked, and I wasn't sure what to do next. I wanted him to ask me to stay. I really felt like, after the missed opportunity on the train and then our reconnection, we had a chance at something big and beautiful and real. I thought maybe my heart was already invested and maybe it had been since the red line train that day. But maybe that was just my hopeless romantic showing. Maybe I'd worn out my welcome and it was time to go. I started to stand. "Well—"

"Will you stay?" Brooks asked in a rush.

I told myself to play it cool as my heart skipped a beat and I said, "I'd love to."

7

———

BROOKS

AN HOUR LATER, we had both taken quick showers and gotten dressed, and I was dishing up the ice cream I'd promised Henry while he sat on my couch scrolling through Netflix.

"Here ya go." I handed Henry a bowl. "Sorry if it's too much."

"No such thing when it comes to ice cream. Or sex."

"I couldn't agree more." A smile tugged at my lips as I took him in. He looked good sitting cross-legged on my couch. Comfy. At home. Like he was where he belonged. *Okay, pump the brakes there, Dr. Bruno. You've been on two dates.* I settled myself onto the couch beside him and dug into my own dessert. "Have you picked anything?" I blatantly ignored his sex remark. I wanted to spend time with Henry, and if I had my way, he'd be spending the night, and maybe the rest of the weekend, with me, and we'd have plenty of time for another round or ten.

"Not yet. I'm torn between *Arrow* and *The Flash.*"

"Definitely *Arrow.*"

"Have you already seen it?" Henry asked.

"Yep, but there is something about Stephen Amell."

He laughed, choking a little on the bite he'd just taken. "Yes.

Yes, there is." I picked up the remote and clicked on the first episode of the first season.

We watched and ate in companionable silence for a little while, and my mind wandered to how surreal it was that I was sitting on my couch with the guy I'd been fascinated by that day on the train. Henry was amazing, and we seemed to have really hit it off. The whole situation—Henry being the bookstore owner my friend had pushed me to go see—felt like the sort of thing that only happened in a rom-com, but if this was my life now, I wasn't going to complain.

"Oh shit," Henry said, and I looked over to see he'd dripped some ice cream onto the shirt he was borrowing and the arm of the couch.

"No big deal. Let me just grab a paper towel."

Henry set his bowl on the coffee table and put an arm out to stop me. "I made the mess. I'll go." He stood and walked toward the kitchen before I could protest that he was my guest. I paused the show, knowing the pull-up scene was coming up and no one should miss that.

My ice cream was nearly gone before I noticed Henry still hadn't come back to the living room. The apartment wasn't big enough for him to have gotten lost. "Henry? Are you okay?"

I grabbed my empty bowl and started toward the kitchen. When I hit the hallway, I realized the door to my office was open. My stomach hit the floor, and the butter pecan I'd just consumed threatened to make a reappearance as guilt crawled up my throat.

"Henry?" My feet carried me over the threshold. Henry stood in the middle of the room with his back to me. He was staring at the wall next to the window where I had framed copies of all my covers on display. There was an eight-by-ten photo of a slightly younger me with my arm thrown around Stacey, my agent, the very first copy of my very first paperback held between us.

This was bad. And goddamn it, Becket was right again. I should have told Henry about my secret identity.

"What is this?" Henry asked, still not looking my way.

"I can explain."

Henry whipped around, and his hands went to his hips.

"I'm not just an English professor," I said, and Henry scoffed. "I also write romantic suspense and mystery novels as R.W. Cook."

"You haven't returned my email."

It took a second for my brain to catch up, and the delay must have shown on my face.

"My last email. The one asking you if you want to book a date to do a reading and a signing." Henry ran a hand through his hair and blew out a big breath. "You know I'm a huge fan." His shoulders sagged. "And now I just feel like an idiot. You already knew what the book was about the day we met." His eyes narrowed. "Why did you really come to Tiny Tales?" Henry crossed his arms over his chest and glared at me.

I deserved it.

The sigh that escaped my lips rivaled any gust the Windy City had ever seen. "First, I told you why I came to the bookstore. My friend was at an event at your shop during Pride. The part I left out was that he'd also shown me the ad you took out in the *Reader* asking for local authors to do readings and signings. He suggested I reach out to you. Honestly, I wasn't going to do it, but he nagged me until I relented. He made me BCC him on the email and everything."

Henry's face fell.

"It's not because I don't want to. It's just… I don't. The university doesn't know I write fiction. A lot of people, my father and my boss for example, think writing genre fiction is beneath someone with a doctorate. I've always just kept the two things very separate. My friend, agent, and publicist, Stacey, keeps bugging me to go to reader conventions and do signings, but I haven't because I'm not sure I want to risk it."

Henry's posture relaxed a fraction. "You don't seem to like teaching all that much, so what's the big deal?"

I wasn't surprised he didn't get it. He hadn't grown up with my dad, esteemed law professor Dr. Anthony Bruno, JD, PhD.

"It's not that simple." I set my empty ice cream bowl on the desk and scrubbed a hand over my face. Henry was staring at me, his brow quirked. I wasn't sure what he saw, but he deflated a little.

"I get why you didn't respond about the signing, and we're going to circle back to that later. Why didn't you tell me? You knew I was a fan." He grimaced. "You let me tell you how excited I was that R.W. Cook had responded to my ad." He sighed and let out a humorless laugh. "Though I guess I know what you look like now."

I couldn't keep a smile from pulling up one side of my mouth. "You probably know what I look like better than anyone else who has read my books."

Henry's cheeks went the cutest shade of pink, and I had no doubt he was remembering our earlier activities. As was I. My dick twitched, but Henry recrossed his arms and my cock stood down.

"You haven't answered my question."

"Again, it's kind of complicated. On the train, when you were so into the book, I was shocked. I'd never seen anyone reading one of my books before, and when you proved you were a fan, I was totally taken aback. And I thought you were cute. And you were willing to talk literature with me. Things got a little fuzzy for me, and it didn't seem to matter." I sighed again. "At your shop, I was surprised it was you. And then we started chatting, and I wanted to see you again, and maybe it's lame, but I wanted you to see me as more than just an author you liked or some guy you were trying to recruit to do a reading at your store." I shrugged and realized I'd delivered most of that to Henry while looking at my feet.

Henry had crossed the room, and he tipped my chin up. "Okay. I can respect that. I'm still a little embarrassed, and don't think just because we're dating now that I'm letting you off the hook about the signing."

"Dating?"

"Yes. Dating."

I smiled and pulled him closer, pressing a quick kiss to his lips. "You're not mad?"

"No. I was at first, but everything you said makes sense. And if you feel that bad, you can do a reading and signing as penance." I scowled, and Henry giggled. "Kidding. But maybe not."

Another kiss to his lips was my only response.

"So, is this where the magic happens?" Henry gestured around the room, sweeping his arm out to indicate my desk.

We had backed up toward the wall as we'd been talking, and I leaned heavily against it, raking my fingers through my hair. I was looking at my feet again because I wasn't exactly sure how to tell Henry the next part. I didn't want to disappoint him.

"Brooks, I'm sorry. I didn't mean to pry. I shouldn't have—"

"No, it's fine." Pushing off the wall, I went to stand behind my desk chair. My plotting notebook sat next to my wireless keyboard. A shudder tried to roll through me when I thought of all the blank pages inside, but I repressed it, hoping Henry wouldn't see.

I turned and took in the room, trying to see the space through Henry's eyes. As the lair of a decently popular writer, I had to imagine he found it rather disappointing. The chair behind the desk was ergonomic but didn't scream comfort. A small bookshelf sat on the other side of the window at the end of the desk, filled with writing craft books. The bottom shelf was empty except for two copies of *The Norton Anthology of American Literature*, which were being used to weight the shelf. A corkboard hung over the short end of my corner desk, but besides the picture of Stacey and me and the framed book covers, there was nothing else on the walls. The room was kind of depressing, utilitarian, uninspiring. Maybe my space was responsible for my lack of creativity, though it had never been an issue in the past.

"Yeah, it's, um, not much but this is where I write. Usually. I, um, haven't written in a while, though. I spent a lot of time in here doing my tenure application this spring, and I just haven't gotten back into the groove yet." I rubbed a hand over the back of my head. "That was another reason I didn't want to tell you who I was. I haven't had a good idea I can work with in months. Since you're a fan, I didn't want to disappoint you if I don't write again."

Henry reached out and put his hand on my shoulder. "Sounds like you're a little burnt out, but you'll get back to writing. You'll find new inspiration."

"God, I hope so. Sometimes I'm afraid I'm forgetting how to write."

Henry grabbed my hand and pulled me toward the door. "It might not be the inspiration you're looking for, but I find Stephen Amell doing the salmon ladder to be quite inspiring."

I laughed, hit the light switch, and shut the door behind us as we walked back to the living room. I was grateful for the distraction. My writer woes could be dealt with another day. "Salmon ladder?"

"Yeah, you know, the jumpy pull-up thing."

"I had no idea that had a name. I've learned something new. Thank you." I pulled Henry in and kissed him on the cheek, then towed him toward the kitchen so we could grab a kitchen towel to clean up the ice cream on the sofa.

His face had gone pink again. "Stick with me and you'll learn all sorts of stuff."

"Of that I have no doubt," I said as we settled back onto the couch and Henry snuggled against me.

8

HENRY

AS WE'D WATCHED a few more episodes of *Arrow*, I hadn't had any idea if Brooks was inspired, but I had been struck by a bolt of inspiration. I knew exactly what I was going to do with the third-floor nook. I was going to turn it into a space for Brooks. Even if we didn't end up working out long-term, which I couldn't imagine after spending one of the best weekends of my life with him. I'd had to open Tiny Tales on Saturday, but I'd spent the rest of the weekend at his apartment, watching movies, cooking together, walking around the neighborhood, and working through the last of Brooks's almost expired condom supply so we wouldn't waste them. It was the environmentally conscious thing to do after all.

Even if things changed, I could see us staying friends. I wanted Brooks in my life—as a friend or more, though more was definitely my preference. He could use the nook to write, and maybe being surrounded by other books in a comfy space would provide him with the inspiration he needed. I couldn't wait to get started, which was why I'd been drawing up plans for the space at my desk for the better part of the morning.

"Whatcha up to, buttercup?" Mrs. Matthews braced her hands

on the edge of the desk and cocked her head, trying to make out what I was drawing upside down.

"I finally came up with an idea for the third floor. I want to turn it into a writer's retreat for Brooks."

Mrs. Matthews's eyes went wide. "Hold the phone. Who is Brooks?"

Oh, right. I'd been so lost in my renovation and design plans, I hadn't filled her in. "Might as well grab a seat. This is a long story."

She settled herself in the chair in front of my desk and watched me with rapt attention. She already knew about the mystery guy I'd met on the train, so I briefly recapped that part, then told her about how he'd come into the shop.

"I knew I should have stayed that night! Damn. I always miss the good stuff."

I shrugged. "That's not even the best part." Her jaw hit the floor when I explained how I found out Brooks was actually R.W. Cook and how I'd come up with the plan to give him a new place to write.

"A few things. Number one, I'm not sure I like that he lied to you." She held up a hand when I tried to interject. "Let me finish. I do understand why he did it, though. I can also respect a guy who has a healthy appreciation for Stephen Amell. Point in his favor. Number two. Do you have a picture? I'm dying to know what this guy looks like."

"Nope, no picture. We've only been on two dates. I think it's too early for selfies."

Mrs. Matthews's tattooed-on eyebrows hit her hairline. "Two dates and you're considering major renovations? But you won't snap a selfie? Are you sure you're not just doing this because he happens to be one of your favorite authors? This Brooks character might have a point."

I considered that for a moment. No. I definitely didn't want to transform the upstairs space just because of who he was. We had a deeper connection. I knew it. I'd felt it when we'd had sex, sure, but even more so when we'd been sitting on the couch eating ice cream and watching TV. It was like my soul had recognized something in his. We clicked. We worked. I had no doubt we had a long future ahead of us. "It's definitely more than that. I know it."

Mrs. Matthews pursed her lips, and she rose from her seat. "Okay. I guess you'd better show me your plans then."

I flipped the notebook I'd been drawing in around and walked her through the ideas I had for the space. She hummed through a few of my plans, then slammed her hands down on the desk. "I gotta see this in real life. It's been a long time since I've been up there."

She was halfway to the stairs by the time I caught up. When we hit the storage space, she turned around. "Walk me through it again."

Pacing out the different areas and ideas, I spent the next twenty minutes making tweaks to my plans, scribbling and erasing lines from my notebook.

"I really want to take this wall down, but I'm not sure the landlord would approve. Do you think it's load-bearing?"

Mrs. Matthews considered the wall in question for a second. "I can't tell. What does your lease say about construction?"

"Huh, I'm really not sure. Maybe I should check."

When we'd done all we could upstairs and had returned to the first floor, I pulled up the electronic copy of the lease while Mrs. Matthews went to retrieve her big blue bag from where she'd left it in the romance room. She plopped it onto the chair she'd been sitting in earlier and rummaged through it, emerging a few seconds later with her readers in their case. Fuchsia glasses perched on her nose, she came around to my side of the desk and read over my shoulder as I perused the document onscreen.

"Well, I don't see anything forbidding construction, do you?"

"Nope, I don't either."

She pointed a wrinkled finger at the screen. "Guess you could call that number there and ask to be sure."

"Oh, I missed that. Good plan." I grabbed my phone from the desk drawer where it usually lived while I was at work. A message notification popped up on the screen when I tapped it.

Brooks: Thinking about you. Hope you're having a great day. When can I see you this week?

A smile tugged at my lips, and Mrs. Matthews rolled her eyes and muttered under her breath about young love.

Me: I'm thinking about you too. Does Wednesday work?
Brooks: Wednesday is perfect! Talk later?
Me: Definitely!

"Gah, I think I'm getting a cavity from that sweet look on your face." Mrs. Matthews made a yuck face but shot me a wink.

I set my phone down and turned back to my computer. What had I been doing?

Mrs. Matthews cleared her throat. "Aren't you forgetting something?"

When whatever I'd been doing before I'd looked at Brooks's message didn't immediately occur to me, she pointed at my phone. "You were going to make a phone call about the renovations."

"Oh, right! Oops, I forgot."

"Henry, lamb chop, we need to work on your ability to multitask."

I stuck my tongue out at her and dialed the number. As the phone rang in my ear, Mrs. Matthews's phone also rang in her bag. She dove in to get it, and when she had it in hand, she ducked around a nearby shelf of Chicago history books to answer it.

"Hello." The voice that answered sounded too familiar.

"Uh, hello. I'm looking for the EWM Family Foundation. My name is Henry Miller. I lease the property at 2129 West Armitage in Chicago."

"Yes, Mr. Miller. How can I help you?" Okay, I definitely knew that voice, and was it my imagination or was I hearing the person on the other end in stereo? Pushing back from my desk, I stood slowly and walked around the shelf where Mrs. Matthews had disappeared. Sure enough, she had her phone pressed to her ear, her back to me.

"I'd like to know if I can tear down a wall on the third floor of the building."

"Hmm. I'd have to look into that." Mrs. Matthews put a hand on the shelf next to her. "What does your lease agreement say?"

I tapped her on the shoulder, and she spun, startled. "It says to call this number," I said into the phone, though Mrs. Matthews's sheepish expression told me everything I needed to know.

"Well, I approve, then." She had the decency to pull the phone away from her ear, and I did the same.

"You've been coming here for five years. Five. Were you ever going to tell me you owned the building?"

Mrs. Matthews drew herself up to her full four-foot-eleven height. "Yes, I was going to tell you when I died, and they called to tell you I'd left you the building."

"That's a little morbid, don't you think?" Something else she'd just said clicked in my brain. "Wait. What do you mean you're leaving me the building?"

"I don't think it's that difficult to comprehend."

"Explain."

"My husband, Edwin William Matthews, left me the building, and thus, it is mine to leave to you."

"But I thought you were on a fixed income?"

Her wrinkled cheeks went a little pink. "Well, technically, I am. It's just more than you might expect."

"But—"

"Honestly, Henry. That bag"—she gestured to the teal monstrosity—"is a Balenciaga. I assumed you knew."

I gaped at her, and she slid a bony finger under my chin to close my mouth.

"The fish-out-of-water look doesn't suit you. Let's go take another look at those plans of yours. I know a guy who might be able to help."

She hustled to the desk, and I had no choice but to follow her. "Must be the week for people dropping big important pieces of information on me."

"Oh, hush. Don't make this a thing." She waved my protest away with a hand in the air between us. She had effectively shut down any continued conversation I wanted to have. It was a lot to process, but Mrs. Matthews directed my attention back to the project at hand. Before I was even sure what was happening, given I was still reeling from the bomb she'd just dropped, she had a contractor scheduled to come in and look at the wall I wanted to take down and had pulled up five different websites featuring flooring, lighting, and paint colors. I wasn't even sure how she'd ended up in my chair.

"Why are you doing all this?"

"All what?"

"This! Everything."

"Well, I made you call the number in the lease because I thought it would be fun to make you work for it a bit." She winked, and I glared.

"And I'm doing this because I can. Because you treat me like family and being here gives me something to do. Because you've been kind to me since the first day I dropped by to meet you. I don't have any kids of my own, and though you'd actually be more like my grandson—ugh, doesn't that make me feel old—I want to." She spun on the seat to face me, her feet barely reaching the floor. "Will it make you happy to make your man happy?"

I wasn't sure I could call Brooks my man just yet, but I nodded anyway, unwilling to engage in another debate with my generous benefactor.

Mrs. Matthews patted my shoulder. "Good. That makes me happy." After a beat, she continued. "If you wanted to make me even happier, you could get me Janet Evanovich's autograph."

A chuckle slipped past my lips, my heart full to bursting with love for the little old lady who'd wandered into my store and never left and the possibility of an amazing future with Brooks and my books.

I had no idea how I would make it happen, but I'd get her that damn autograph if it was the last thing I did.

9

BROOKS

THE FALL SEMESTER had started in a blur of campus construction and new course assignments, which included teaching night classes three nights a week, so even though Henry and I had still been spending a lot of time together, I hadn't had time to visit him at work since the academic year had started.

Over the summer, since my first trip to the shop, I'd made it a point to be there whenever I could. Tiny Tales was warm and inviting. Seeing Henry in his element made me happy in a way I didn't quite understand. It was like his joy and love for his shop somehow leaked into me whenever I was there with him, and the feeling made my chest feel like an overinflated balloon stretched tight with contentment. With the drudgery of the new school year well underway, I needed a little of that feeling. I'd been missing it.

Finally, on a day in mid-September, Dr. Butler canceled our monthly faculty meeting, and I was able to escape the chaos of campus earlier than normal. It was the perfect day to surprise Henry with a visit.

I walked up to Armitage and grabbed the 73 bus that would

take me to Wicker Park. The sun was shining, the leaves were changing colors, and there was a hint of cooler weather in the air. Everything around me screamed change, and as I looked at my relationship with Henry over the past month, I couldn't help but feel like all signs were pointing to a change for the better.

The bus bumped along the potholed streets that hadn't made the summer repair docket as I pulled out my earbuds and cued up a fiction podcast I loved. I thought about how adorable Henry had been the week before when we'd met Beckett for dinner at the Hopleaf in Andersonville after our respective late classes on Thursday night.

Beckett had insisted on making a big deal about how reaching out to Henry had been all his idea. Henry had swooned at the serendipity of the thing, and I'd had to steady him on his barstool, though honestly, I blamed the high-alcohol beer he'd selected then chugged, citing nerves over meeting my friend. The story of how we met was pretty epic. If Henry was going to give me the win, it would be rude not to take it. Beckett hadn't stopped teasing me about it since, but I vowed to one day get my revenge when he met someone as perfect for him as Henry was for me.

The bus was approaching my stop, so I paused my podcast since I hadn't been listening that intently anyway and stowed my earbuds. I straightened my tie and rerolled my shirt sleeves. Someone else had already pushed the stop request button, so I rose from my seat and moved to the back of the bus. As we approached the stop, we passed Tiny Tales, and I caught a fleeting glimpse through the bus's window. It was a tiny row house nestled between two heavily remodeled modern buildings. A little piece of Chicago's past stuck in modern time.

As I walked from the bus stop, I looked in the big front window. The display was fall festive, but interspersed among the crimson-and-gold foliage were stacks of books by local and national Hispanic and Latinx authors under a banner celebrating Hispanic Heritage Month. The titles in the window ran the gamut from poetry to romance to historical nonfiction to contemporary political commentary.

My phone rang just as I reached out to open the door.

Fuck. I'd been dodging calls from my dad since the beginning of the semester. It wasn't to the point he would leave his cushy Evanston home to venture to the city and track me down yet, but that time was fast approaching. If I answered now, I could avoid him showing up at my apartment—or worse at MacMillan—and at least Henry would be right there to comfort me.

I took a few deep breaths and tapped the screen to accept the call. "Hi, Dad."

"Brooks. You've been avoiding my calls."

"Just been busy."

"With what? I spoke with Armin. Your course load isn't that heavy."

That was a lie. I was teaching more courses than any of the other adjuncts because Dr. Butler had said it would be beneficial for the tenure committee to see me taking on a more substantial workload. I still wasn't sure why I had agreed or why my father insisted on interfering with my boss, regardless of how close they'd been as pledges in Psi Mu Delta. "I'm teaching five classes."

"Yes, but three of them are only one night per week."

"Dad, each of those classes is three hours long."

"You're never going to get tenure if you don't step up."

"I'm not sure I even want tenure." Shit. I hadn't meant for that to slip out.

The silence on the other end of the line was deafening, but there was no way to walk back what I'd just said even if I'd wanted to, so I let it hang between us.

"Your mother—"

"No. She's been gone for more than twenty years. You don't get to use her passion for academia, or your own, to make me feel guilty. Mom loved being in the field. Maybe I'll do something like that."

My dad sputtered. "What would that even look like? Your doctorate is in English literature. Teaching *is* being in the field for you."

"I could write." In that moment, I wanted to confess that I'd never given it up. "I am writing."

"Brooks, I thought we spoke about this."

"You spoke and assumed I listened." The sudden show of backbone where my father was concerned was a shock. I had never contradicted him like this before. Henry and I had had a lot of conversations about my family recently. Maybe talking about my relationship with my dad and the memories of my mom had shaken something loose. Henry had told me he was certain my mom would have wanted me to be happy. I didn't realize until that moment that I'd taken his words to heart.

"Brooks—"

"I'm not making any decisions, but I am exploring my options. I get to decide what I want to do, what makes me happy."

My dad made a tutting noise. "What a waste of a perfectly good PhD. You are—"

It was probably a little immature, but I hung up before he could tell me how disappointed he was. I still hadn't been able to find a new idea I could work with for my next book, and I refused to think about how my confession that I was writing might have been a little premature. His negativity would just further fuel my own self-doubt.

I paced in front of Tiny Tales for a second, trying to get back to the headspace I'd been in on the way over. I should have ignored the call. Too late now. I shook out my hands and tried to shrug off the tension in my shoulders that always accompanied a conversation with my father.

Looking for a distraction, I spotted the LGBTQ Pride and Human Rights Campaign stickers proudly displayed on the door.

I'd never noticed them before, probably because I'd always been distracted by Henry, and when we came to the shop together, we usually entered through the back. Another sticker announced that Tiny Tales was a member of the LGBT Chamber of Commerce Illinois and the LGBTQ Booksellers and Librarians Association. Henry had done an amazing job making his store a safe space, and not for the first time since we'd gotten together, the thought of taking him up on his offer to do a reading and signing flashed through my mind. He'd been good about not bringing it up too often, only about once a week, and I had to admit I was softening toward the idea.

Bells jingled as I crossed the threshold and the door swung shut behind me. The sound settled something in my chest, as did the sound of Henry's voice coming from the back of the shop.

"Mrs. Matthews, I know you like what you like, but sometimes I can get a better deal on a different brand."

"You're right, sweet pea. I like what I like, and as your best customer, you'd think you'd want to keep me happy," a second voice, this one older, female, and slightly raspy, replied. I assumed since Henry had addressed her as Mrs. Matthews, that it was her voice that had responded.

"You have to buy something to be a customer. You just read my books, drink my coffee, and use my toilet paper."

"Oh, please, Henry. I add interest to this place. Everything is so taupe here without me. Besides, you need my marketing ingenuity."

They continued to bicker, and I took in everything I loved about the shop, which further settled my disquiet. I thought about all the nooks I'd discovered over the summer and longed to find a spot to curl up in for a second. The room smelled like new books, old building, oil soap, and a hint of Henry's clean citrus cologne, and I breathed in a huge lungful, letting it replace the last of the tightness in my chest.

The window display poured into the room onto a table filled

with additional copies of the books in the window as well as others, and I passed down the aisle between shelves, examining the new titles Henry was stocking to honor Hispanic voices.

At the end of the row, I looked up and then jumped back when I encountered a petite gray-haired lady in a neon purple nylon tracksuit in front of me. The elusive Mrs. Matthews, I presumed. She was usually gone for the day by the time I'd gotten there during the summer, and she apparently didn't come in often on Saturdays. I almost screamed but held it together. Where had she come from? Also, I was ninety-nine percent sure a person couldn't move in that material without making noise unless they were part ninja.

"Henry! I think you'd better get out here. You have a customer, and he is hot. As in hot with two *t*'s." She never took her eyes off me as she relayed these details to Henry in the other room, and she looked at me over her fuchsia reading glasses as though she might consider taking me home if Henry wasn't interested.

"Mrs. Matthews! I've told you a hundred times, you can't talk about the cust—" Henry's voice had been getting louder as he moved toward us, but he stopped talking abruptly when he saw me. He ran the last few steps, threw himself into my arms, and planted a kiss on my cheek.

"Brooks! Oh my god. What are you doing here? I didn't know you were coming by today," Henry said, releasing me from his hug. I kept one arm around his waist because I just wanted to touch him. God, being near him was like being home.

"I got out earlier than expected. Canceled faculty meeting, so I figured I'd pop by. Is that okay?" I asked.

"That's perfect." Henry reached up to kiss me again and the kiss was just about to go from friendly to more-than-friendly when a staccato beat and the clearing of a throat had us pulling apart. We turned to see Mrs. Matthews tapping her leopard-print sneaker, hands on her hips. Neither of us said anything, and Mrs. Matthews just looked at us, waiting for some sort of explanation.

When she clearly could wait no longer, she said, "For god's sake, Henry. Introduce me."

Henry rolled his eyes, sighed, and rested his forehead against mine for a second before he pulled away and said, "Mrs. Matthews, Brooks. Brooks, Mrs. Matthews. Now will you please go back to your book?"

She ignored him, stepping forward with an outstretched hand.

"It's nice to meet you, Mrs. Matthews. I've heard so much about you," I said, pushing out of Henry's arms and clasping her wrinkled hand in mine.

"Ah, strong hands. I like that." She held my hand between both of hers and looked at me intently. "Do you know Janet Evanovich?"

"Um… who?" My hand fell to my side as she released it unexpectedly.

"Henry, are you sure he's a legitimate author? He doesn't know Janet. I have concerns."

Tears of mirth gathered in my eyes, and I raised my hand to cover a laugh. No wonder Henry loved this woman. She was a riot.

"Mrs. Matthews! Go back to the other room. I can't believe you would say something so rude."

"You know I call it like I see it, Henry." Henry put his hands on her shoulders and turned her gently. When she started walking away, grumbling the whole way about how people she helped should have more respect, Henry turned to me.

"I am so sorry—wait. Are you laughing?"

"I think I'm in love. She's the best. I totally get why you like her so much."

Henry rolled his eyes and flopped into his chair behind his desk. "Shh." Henry motioned for me to lower my voice. "Don't let her hear you say that. Also, you like her now, but she's like this every day. Don't worry, though. I have a plan." There was a glint in Henry's eyes I hadn't seen before, and I had a feeling it spelled trouble for Mrs. Matthews.

"Henry, she's like eighty years old."

"She's seventy-eight, and there is no excuse for that kind of behavior."

I chuckled again. "I should probably maintain plausible deniability, but I'm dying to know what you're plotting."

"I'm going to change the toilet paper in the bathroom from Charmin to Angel Soft. She hates Angel Soft. It'll drive her crazy. Well, crazier. She's already bananas."

I laughed again, and it took me a long time to pull myself together.

Henry followed through on his plan, but it didn't last long as Mrs. Matthews paid him back in kind by bringing in her own rolls of Charmin and carrying them back and forth to the bathroom with her.

He promptly removed the offending brand, and things returned to normal.

10

BROOKS

October

FUCK. Fuckity fuck, fuck, fuck.

I stared at the blinking cursor on the top of the blank page. It was mocking me with its cheerful winking.

"Fuck you, cursor, and fuck you, blank page," I muttered as I shot my computer the double bird.

No new ideas. Not one. My creative well had run dry. I was a wasteland of dying prose. The few glimmers of creative thought I'd had in the last five months lay dead and picked over in a graveyard of discarded Word documents. My proverbial garbage can was overflowing with balled-up examples of writing even a kindergartener would sneer at.

I pushed my keyboard back and thunked my head on my desk. My muses had left me here to die. I bounced my forehead on the desk's surface as I contemplated my fate.

That stupid phone call with my dad last week was no doubt to blame. I'd had the spark of an idea, but after I'd told him I was writing and alluded to making a go of it full-time, it had been snuffed out.

Fuck.

Five months had passed since my last release, and I hadn't successfully put pen to paper since. One hundred fifty-two days of creative drought and counting. If I couldn't get my shit together soon, Stacey would start dropping more than the casual curious question about my latest work in progress. And Henry... Things were going so well, but if I never produced another novel, would he still be interested in me? Maybe he was just dating me because I was an author. *Wow, dramatic much, Dr. Bruno?*

I rolled my head to the side, pressing my unshaven cheek against the cold and unforgiving surface of my desk, and stared out my office window through the spaces in my miniblinds. Henry had seemed to have more or less given up on me doing a signing at Tiny Tales, but last night after a particularly spectacular blow job, he'd asked again, and in a haze of postorgasmic bliss, I'd agreed. What was I going to do? Surely if I went through with the signing, people would ask about my next book, and I would have nothing to say because I was working on nothing.

Maybe I just needed to get away. I hadn't left the city in months. Maybe a change of scenery, a long weekend away with Henry and hotel sex to reset my brain. But shit, the semester was already in full swing, and as much as I wanted to leave my current batch of underperforming coeds to their own devices, that wouldn't help my case for tenure. Though I was at the point where I was ninety percent sure I no longer cared. But if I wasn't teaching and I wasn't writing, what was I going to do? Residual royalties could only carry me so far.

Fuck. I rolled my head again and resumed bouncing my forehead off the desk, hoping to shake an idea loose.

The desktop began to vibrate as my phone rang somewhere near my left ear. The vibration pulled me just far enough out of my pit of self-pity and self-loathing to grope blindly for the phone. I brought it to my ear without checking the display or removing my head from the desk.

"Hello," I said, my voice muffled by despair.

"Brooks?" Henry said with concern. "Are you okay?"

I sat up and massaged my forehead with the heel of my hand. I flipped the phone to speaker and set it on my desk while I threw myself back in my desk chair in a completely melodramatic fashion.

"Hey, Henry. I'm fine." Lie.

"Okay…" He didn't sound convinced.

"What's going on? Everything okay with you? All good at the shop?"

"Oh, yeah. Everything is great here. Business as usual."

"Great."

"Uh, yep. Hey, I actually wanted to talk to you about last night."

Kill me now. "Oh, uh, sure."

"Are you really okay with doing a small appearance?"

This was the out I needed, but I couldn't bring myself to disappoint Henry by taking it. "Uh, sure. Why wouldn't I be?"

"Well, you kind of agreed under duress after weeks of saying no."

"Duress?"

"Um…"

"Henry, I'm not sure my dick in your mouth counts as duress."

He giggled, and I pictured the rosy blush that was no doubt staining his cheeks. "I swear I wasn't trying to manipulate you to agree, but I did tell you I planned to be persuasive."

"That you did."

"Uh, so anyway, I was hoping we could nail down a date."

Shit. "Nail down a date, hmm?" I asked, stalling for time and hoping to get my stomach from off the floor where it had plummeted.

"Yeah. I'm thinking sometime in early December."

Seriously, fuck my life. "December?" On second thought,

December was two months away. I could get out of this funk by then. *Oh god, please let that be true.*

"Yep. The first or second week of the month maybe?"

I pulled my leather workbag out from under my desk and rummaged in it for my planner. I flipped to December. "Finals are the second week, so the first week would work." I was almost positive this whole experience was going to be torture, but I lo— really liked—Henry, and this would make him happy, so... Besides, if I was really going to bid academic life adieu, I would need to get used to this stuff. I would no longer have an excuse to avoid it.

"Awesome! I'm going to get started on flyers and a banner for the website right now. This is so exciting!"

Henry's enthusiasm was palpable even through the phone, and I smiled in spite of the shitstorm that was my life. "I'm happy you're happy."

"Oh! What are you going to read? Something new maybe?" I'd been purposefully cagey when Henry had asked about my writing, though he knew it hadn't been going well.

"Um…" I oscillated back and forth in my chair like an impotent desk fan while I tried to think of how I was going to explain my lack of new material to the man who might be the love of my life.

"I get it," Henry said. "It's a tough decision. You don't have to commit yet."

Thank god. "It's not that"—I turned the chair again and caught sight of *Kryptonite* on my bookshelf—"I just thought I'd read from *Kryptonite* since it's your favorite, and it's what you were reading when we met."

Henry's swoony squeak would have pierced a lesser man's eardrums. "Oh my god! That is the most romantic thing ever. I love… that idea. Yes! *Kryptonite* it is!"

"Perfect." I let out a long breath. At least we'd always have *Kryptonite*, even if I never wrote again.

"Well, I'll let you get back to work. I've got to-do lists to create for the signing. I'm so excited, Brooks. Thank you so much for doing this."

"Anything for you, babe." And I meant it. Making Henry happy was one of my favorite things.

"I'll see you later, right?"

"Definitely." Henry was the only glimmer of light in my otherwise bleak existence. Ugh, maybe I was getting a little morose even for myself.

"See you soon."

"Yep. See you soon." I clicked End and thunked my head against the desk again. *Two months, Brooks. You've got two months to figure your shit out. Get to it.*

11

HENRY

NOVEMBER

"MRS. MATTHEWS, hand me the Allen wrench." I was sitting in the third-floor nook surrounded by boxes from IKEA. Mrs. Matthews had insisted she was a master carpenter and had appointed herself my assistant, but outside of handing me a few smaller pieces and the occasional tool, she hadn't done much more than sit and harass me about my relationship with Brooks.

Things had been a little weird between us after she'd told me she owned the building, but she'd explained in no uncertain terms she wouldn't have it. Her exact words had been, "Henry, you'd better get your head out of your ass about this. I won't stand for it." And that had been that. I'd made sure she knew everything was okay when I'd replaced her favorite toilet paper with her least favorite brand after she'd met Brooks in person for the first time. I had no regrets, and things were back to as normal as they'd ever been between us.

"Coming up, buttercup." She dug in the pockets of the Crafty Beaver nail apron she was wearing and pulled out a Phillips-head screwdriver, a bunch of little wooden dowels, and finally the Allen wrench I needed.

"Thanks," I said as she passed it over and motioned for me to give her the instructions I was holding.

"Henry, my dear, how do you read this?" she asked, sliding her fuchsia readers up and down on her nose.

I rolled my eyes. "You don't read anything. You look at the pictures. It's like furniture LEGOs."

She harrumphed and sat in the plush chair she'd helped me pick out—and insisted on buying—for Brooks's writing space.

I'd spent the past months planning and purchasing things to fill the nook in between events at the shop and running the day-to-day business. Several local authors had already done readings and signings, and the events had been really successful. Drag Queen Story Hour had been featured on the news in an around-town segment, and since then we'd had to add an extra date every month to keep up with the demand. The children's section was getting a lot of use, and I loved it. As much as I teased Mrs. Matthews, I would never have come up with those ideas without her, and the extra traffic was making a huge difference in the year-over-year figures. It had been an insanely busy fall.

Brooks had been really busy too. His classes were kicking his butt, and he'd had a couple meetings with the tenure committee to review aspects of his CV before the formal interviews that were set to take place in January. We'd had a lot of conversations about what he wanted from his future, but with his writing not as on track as he wanted it to be and his dad breathing down his neck, I knew he felt like he'd been painted into a corner. Hopefully, the new space would help him make a decision about what to do next.

The construction crew Mrs. Matthews had hired had been in for the last two weeks, and they had torn down the wall I wanted moved, put in new flooring, and added some electrical outlets. They'd also painted, and the walls were now a soothing pale gray.

It had been easy to have items delivered and to haul IKEA boxes upstairs until Brooks had started hanging out at Tiny Tales more often. Now I had to work on the sly, and I had reminders set on my phone for his last classes so I'd know when I had to pack it up for the day just in case he stopped in. I'd also installed an alarm on the door to the shop that chimed every time someone opened it so I could run downstairs and greet customers. I was definitely getting a daily workout running up and down, but I wanted the space to be done before Christmas. I couldn't wait to surprise Brooks.

"You're humming that song again," Mrs. Matthews said from her spot in the comfy chair.

I finished tightening the screw I was working on and looked up at her. "What song?"

"The one from that Disney movie." She hummed, finding her pitch, and sang, "So this is love, mmm, mmm, mmm."

I made a face. "You're a little pitchy."

"I am not," she said throwing the instruction book back at me. "But is it?"

"Is what, what?"

She pushed her glasses to the tip of her nose and looked at me over them. "I swear, you're gonna drive me to drink, Henry Miller. Is. It. Love?"

I felt my cheeks go pink, and I turned away to grab the instruction manual to figure out what pieces I needed next. When I was done with this project, I was never setting foot in IKEA again. Though there had been that really cute set of end tables. Maybe just one more time. Brooks could help me put them together.

"Aha! I knew it!" Mrs. Matthews declared.

"You know nothing. I was thinking about end tables I saw at IKEA during my last trip out there."

Mrs. Matthews glared at me over her readers. "Well, that's a lie. No one smiles like that"—she made fast circles with her gnarled pointer finger encompassing my face—"thinking about furniture."

"They're very nice end tables."

She cocked her head and pursed her lips. "Henry…"

Defeated, I slumped back and slid down the wall. "Don't you think it's a little early to be using the L-word? I mean, it's only been four months. It's way too soon to be thinking about love." I picked up the instruction booklet for the desk and thumbed through it absently. "Right?"

"Sugar plum, if your girl Cinderella could fall in love in one night, then I think four months is more than enough time. Have you told him?"

"Are you even listening to me? I just said it's too early to be making big declarations."

Mrs. Matthews glared at me over her glasses again. "Well, one of you has to make a move, and you're the one sitting in front of me at the moment, so you get the lecture. If you love him, tell him. I have a feeling if you're waiting for Brooks to say it first, you'll be waiting until I'm eighty."

A slightly manic giggle tumbled out. "Isn't that only like a year and a half from now?"

"Pfft. Never ask a lady her age."

"I didn't. You brought it up." Pulling the pieces I needed for one of the desk drawers my way, I averted my attention and focused on the next step.

"Fine, but don't think I don't see what you're doing."

"Oh?" I slid the bottom into the drawer and set it aside. I was almost done with the desk. Just a few more steps and I could add the legs and set it in place.

"Henry, focus." I heard her shuffle out of the chair to stand in front of me. I had no choice but to look up at her, lest I be blinded by her neon sneakers.

"You need to tell Brooks how you feel. Even though I don't think he's a real author, he's still a good man. And he makes you happy."

I rolled my eyes. "I'm not having this conversation with you again."

"What?" She affected a look of innocence. "There's no picture in his books, and he doesn't know Janet Evanovich. He told me he'd never even heard of her. Can you believe it? That's like saying he doesn't know Danielle Steel or Nora Roberts. Oh, I should ask him if he knows them."

"He doesn't write romance," I singsonged for what had to be the six millionth time.

She dismissed my comment with an imperious wave. "Back to what I was saying before you interrupted. You need to tell your man how you feel. I'll bug you until you do it. I'm good at that."

"Oh, I know you are." She slapped me lightly on the shoulder and muttered something that sounded a little like *asshole* under her breath. "I'm hoping creating this space for him says it for me."

"Hmm, that might work." She tapped her foot. "But you know what might work even better? Talking. To. Him."

Attention back on the drawer, I ignored her.

"I get the feeling you aren't hearing me." She nudged a piece of the next drawer toward me with her toe.

"I hear you. I'm just not listening. Also, just because Brooks doesn't know Janet Evanovich or Danielle Steel doesn't mean he's not a real author. Writing is kind of a solitary thing."

"Uh-huh. Though I guess he is doing the signing here soon, right? If people are coming to hear him read, he must be legit."

I snorted. "I'm pretty sure he's legit, Mrs. Matthews. You've seen his books."

She waved a hand like she was shooing away a fly. "But how do we really *know* it's him? There's no picture!"

"Oh, for heaven's sake. We've been through this." I flipped the top of the desk over and started screwing in one of the legs.

"All right, all right. Don't get your knickers in a knot." She shuffled back to the chair. "You deserve good things, Henry. And for what it's worth, I think Brooks loves you too."

I choked and then cleared my throat. "Do you really think so?"

"I really do. You told me he's never done a signing before, but he's doing one here. For you. I think that's love."

I thought about that for a minute. Brooks had said the thought of a signing always made him nervous, but even the first time I'd asked, he'd told me he'd think about it. It really hadn't taken much to convince him. Maybe Mrs. Matthews was right. Maybe the signing was Brooks's way of telling me he loved me, just like creating this space for him was mine. Maybe actions really did speak louder than words.

I finished screwing in the last leg and stood from where I'd been sitting. I levered the desk up and scooted it noisily into the corner.

"Henry," Mrs. Mathews said as I wiped down the desktop, "you're humming again."

A smile spread across my face. "Well, this just might be love."

She winked and patted my shoulder. "Atta buy."

12
————

BROOKS

December

BEFORE I KNEW IT, Thanksgiving was over, and I was staring December and the signing at Tiny Tales in the face. Henry had the whole thing orchestrated so I'd read from *Kryptonite*, then sign books for any attendees, provided they purchased the books from the shop. Henry had been deep into planning the event for weeks and was incredibly excited. I was more nervous. For myself because I would potentially be meeting more fans face-to-face, and for Henry because I was afraid no one would show up. Ever the optimist, Henry shared no such concerns and had been planning for a packed house, researching fire codes in case we had too many people.

He'd even ordered extra copies of my books, which had piqued Stacey's curiosity when the orders had shown up on the sales reports she received. I'd had to explain about the signing. And I'd had to endure her excited squealing followed by a stern lecture about "keeping shit like this" from her. I'd promised to send her a box of Vosges chocolates as recompense.

"Are you all set for tonight?" I asked as I filled a travel mug with coffee and got ready to head out to teach my early class.

Henry consulted the checklist and spreadsheet in front of him on the kitchen table. "I think so. I have pastries on order that will be delivered around five and plenty of coffee supplies at the shop already." Henry had been staying at my place almost every night recently, and I liked seeing him comfortable in my space. I had a feeling we'd be having a conversation about living arrangements soon, and I was looking forward to seeing him in the apartment full time. I was trying to decide if giving him a key on a new key ring and a copy of the lease was cliché—the jury was still out.

"Sounds good. I'll be at the shop after my office hours around four. I'll call when I'm on my way, and I can pick up any last-minute stuff you need."

"Thank you." Henry kissed me as I zipped into my coat. "And thank you again for doing this. It really means a lot to me."

I shrugged, feigning nonchalance and ignoring the lead boulder that had landed in my stomach when I woke up that morning. "You're welcome. Stacey has been trying to get me to go to signings since I started writing. I'm not sure who is happier about this, you or her."

"You should listen to your agent. She's smart."

"Yeah, yeah." I kissed Henry again and left to face the day, hoping like hell tonight went well… for both of us.

———

I'D BE LYING if I said I wasn't surprised by the number of people packed into Tiny Tales that night. I had expected maybe ten people, but it seemed like there were more than forty packed into the teeny space. I couldn't even see all the faces of the attendees from where I was seated in Mrs. Matthews's chintz throne at the rear of the romance section. Henry had apparently done some marketing to the local universities' LGBTQ groups, and there were a number of younger faces in the crowd. I didn't see any of my own students, thank god, but with the crush of people it didn't mean they weren't there.

When I'd agreed to do the signing, I had come to terms with my pen name getting out and word getting back to the university, and I would deal with the consequences if they came. This meant so much to Henry, and it made me happy to make him so happy. Besides, my writing was a part of who I was, and I was tired of hiding it. Now if only I could find a little inspiration so I could get back to it. Luckily, Stacey hadn't started breathing down my neck about that just yet. I would have to worry about it later.

It was time for the reading before the signing, and I had selected a passage from *Kryptonite* where the Superman character has been tied up by the Lex Luthor character in a chamber where the walls are lined with kryptonite. Lex just wants Superman to listen, but there is definite sexual tension between the men, and Superman realizes, in his kryptonite-induced haze, that he might have a little bit of a thing for Lex. The story wasn't technically a romance, but the relationship between the two characters was a theme throughout, and Henry said it was his favorite part of the story.

After the reading, I took questions, mostly about my inspiration and why I became a writer, and then I moved to a small table near Henry's desk so he could ring up purchases while I signed books. Once the signing was done, Henry and I mingled with the remaining attendees over pastries and coffee, and before I knew it, it was almost nine thirty. The event had started at six. Henry locked the door behind Mrs. Matthews, who of course was the last to leave, and pulled the rolling shade on the door. He hit the dimmer on the lights and a muted glow was cast over the room. Then he turned to me with an exhausted but happy smile.

"That was amazing! *You* were amazing!" he exclaimed, throwing his arms around my neck and kissing me deeply.

I blushed as he pulled away. "I'm really happy so many people came. It was good for the shop."

"It was good for you too. I almost sold out of all your books. I think I have one copy of *Kryptonite* left in the whole store."

"I guess that's good." Maybe there really was something to this public-appearances thing. Stacey was going to be intolerable when she found out the night had been a success.

"That's a great thing! Speaking of, when are you releasing your next book? Several of the attendees tonight asked me, and I realized I didn't know." I took a step back and paced away from Henry. I ran both hands through my hair, messing up the style, and gave a frustrated sigh.

"That makes two of us. I still haven't really been writing much lately. I've dabbled with a few new ideas, but nothing is really sticking, and I'm not sure they're that great. Nothing is grabbing me like it did for my other books. I know I've said this before, and it's dumb, but it's like the energy has changed in my office." Stacey had told me to "build a bridge and get over it," but that was proving to be easier said than done, and I had a folder full of barely started manuscripts to show for my failed attempts.

Henry smiled an odd smile and said, "I think I understand, and I'm sure an opportunity will present itself. For now, what do you say we celebrate the success of tonight's event?"

"What did you have in mind?" I asked as Henry wound his arms around my neck again and backed me toward the romance section.

"Well, I've been half-hard since you started reading, and I contemplated kicking everyone out when you got to the part where Alex tells Kent he's into tying up his partners."

"Yeah?"

"There was a college kid near the front who started looking at you like he wanted you to take him home and tie him up, and I'll admit, I wanted to punch him a little."

"Aww, babe. You know I only have eyes for you. Besides,

you're a lover, not a fighter, but let's talk more about this previously unmentioned interest in bondage." I gave him my best interested-for-academic-purposes-only look, and he blushed then hid his face in his hands. I didn't mind since it gave me an extra second to take him in. Henry had been a festive vision in a Christmas plaid button-down and dark-green khakis, and my eyes really had been drawn to him constantly throughout the evening.

"Maybe later. I have other ideas for tonight." Henry leaned into me and pressed his lips to mine. I ran my hands up to his head and tunneled my fingers into his curls. I loved the texture of the silky strands and loved to grab them whenever I had the chance. He moaned into my mouth and his hands slid down to my waistband. He opened the clasp, then caressed my length through the thin fabric of my dress pants. The heat of his hand and the perfect pressure had my cock at full attention in no time.

"There's something I've always wanted to do," he said as he lowered my zipper and slid my pants and boxer briefs down.

"Anything," I said, toeing off my shoes and socks. "But I think you have a few too many clothes on at the moment."

Henry giggled and pulled his wallet from his back pocket. "You lose that shirt. I'll handle this." He gestured at himself while I started in on the buttons of my dress shirt.

When my shirt lay discarded on the floor with the rest of my clothes, I noticed Henry had set a condom and a packet of lube on a bookshelf behind Mrs. Matthews's chintz armchair and was standing naked in front of it.

"Come over here," he said, beckoning to me with his eyes and gorgeous body. After a quick check to make sure we couldn't be seen from the street, I was more than happy to comply.

"Kneel on the chair. Ass out, arms on the back," Henry said and again, I was more than happy to obey, hoping I knew where this was going. When I was in position, I heard Henry move behind me.

He ran a hand over my ass, and I shuddered. "You say I have a terrific ass, but I think yours is spectacular too." I felt him move, then I felt a sharp sting as his teeth sank into my right butt cheek. I yelped, and he used his lips to soothe away the bite, his breath ghosting along my crease.

"I've been dying to do that." His fingers traced my crack and pressed against my rim as his other hand spread my cheeks apart. He pressed a kiss to the base of my spine, right above my crease, then changed the pressure and sucked up a bruise to mark the spot. A shudder rolled through me.

"God, this ass. I want to taste it, Brooks. I need to. May I?"

Rimming, both giving and receiving, was one of my favorite things. "Yessss. Yes, please," I said as I hissed out on a sigh. Henry fluttered his fingers over my hole again, and I tensed for a moment as I waited for what I knew was coming next. The first swipe of his tongue around my rim had me gripping the back of the chair and rocking forward. A second stronger swipe had me rocking back and seeking more contact. My cock twitched against my stomach. As Henry licked and used his tongue to delve into my hole, he reached between my legs to tease my balls, pulling them gently and rolling them in his palm. He teased the underside of my cock and pressed his thumb against my taint until I was torn between thrusting into the chair and rocking back into his mouth.

"Henry, please. Please. More," I begged.

"I thought you'd never ask, Professor."

I heard the crinkle of foil as Henry opened the condom and lube and felt the slick press of two of his fingers as he stretched me, picking up where his fucking talented tongue had left off.

"Now, please."

"I've got you, baby," he said as he lined up, and I felt his warm cock slide into me.

He set a quick pace, and I knew from the stutter in his thrusts that he was as strung out and ready to come as I was. In this position, he was hitting me just right on every thrust, and he'd barely reached around to grab my cock when I gasped out a broken "Coming" before spilling into his hand. Henry thrust twice more and groaned as he came, then collapsed against my back, biting at my shoulder.

"That was everything I imagined it would be," he said as he pulled out and tied off the condom, then cleaned up as best he could with some napkins left over from the event.

I laughed and tried to stop but couldn't. Henry looked at me like I'd lost my mind and raised an eyebrow in question.

"I'm just thinking about how I used to think of this as Mrs. Matthews's throne, but now it will forevermore be the sex chair." Henry looked aghast for a second, then burst into his own peals of laughter.

"Oh my god, I will never be able to look at her sitting in this chair the same way again." I grabbed Henry's hand and pulled him in for a kiss and he landed in my lap. "Why didn't I think of that before? That's it—I'm going to have to get rid of it."

"No! You can't. Long live the sex chair!"

13

———

BROOKS

THE NEXT WEEK was finals week, and the finals schedule meant there were different colleagues around the department than usual. It was nice to see people I typically only saw at faculty meetings bustling in and out of their offices. Or so I thought.

I stopped into the faculty workroom to check my department mailbox after proctoring my Twentieth Century American Literature exam, and one of my colleagues, Dr. Claire DeAngelo, grabbed my arm. Claire was an associate professor in the gender studies program and taught a few courses that were cross-listed with English.

"Brooks! Why didn't you tell me you were R.W. Cook?" she said at a volume I would not consider a whisper.

I felt some of the color drain from my face, and I did my best to hide a grimace. She must have been at the signing. Her next words confirmed as much.

"Your reading last week was fantastic, but my partner, Andrea, had the flu, so I had to scoot right after and didn't get a chance to say hello."

"I… um… haven't really been too open about it around here,"

99

I finally managed, glancing over my shoulder to see who might be in the mailroom to overhear.

"Why not? I think it's amazing you're an author," Claire said, clearly not understanding my predicament.

"Who is an author?" a voice I knew and loathed asked from behind us. My stomach hit my feet. My day had just gone from pleasant to not so much in the blink of an eye with five nasal syllables. I turned to see Dr. Armin Butler looking at us with a skeptical expression as he shoved his hands into the pockets of his tweed—fucking tweed—jacket and rocked back on his heels. Exactly the person, and the reason, I hadn't wanted to bring R.W. Cook to work. And only part of it had to do with my tenure application. The other part was solely because he was such close friends with my dad.

Before I could do damage control, Claire started talking. "Brooks! He writes novels with heavy LGBTQ themes. I've used a few in my Gender Topics in Literature and Film course. I love his writing. His books are full of classical and contemporary allusions, and I find his writing to be quite allegorical."

Well, at least she'd made my books sound smart, though if Dr. Butler started searching, he would find Claire was being generous. I had a feeling the explicit on-page sex in the books I'd written might negate any literary value in his eyes.

"Interesting. Dr. Bruno, I'd like you to provide me with a list of your published works and all your pen names as part of your tenure track application by end of day today," Dr. Butler said in the adenoidal voice that brooked no argument.

Shit, damn, and hell. "Of course." Dr. Butler turned and left the workroom without another word, no doubt to call my father. Fuck.

Claire had the decency to look contrite. "I probably shouldn't have said anything, huh?"

"Maybe not." I bit my tongue to keep from saying more. I had never harbored homicidal tendencies, but I was suddenly thinking I could do damage to Claire's person with the blade of the paper cutter on the table behind her, and the last thing I needed was to make any sort of threat in that direction.

"I'm sorry, Brooks. I forgot you're up for a tenure position. I just got really excited, and I really do love your books and use them in class."

"It's okay. We'll see what happens." And we would see, because at that point, what choice was there?

Claire gave my arm a squeeze and left me in the workroom. I collected my mail and turned to head to my office to draw up the list for Dr. Butler.

My phone buzzed with a call from my father before I even made it out the door.

I didn't answer.

———

I WAS GRADING final exams in my office the next day when I got the summons to Dr. Butler's office that I'd been expecting. My dad had left me six voice mail messages—none of which I'd listened to—and I had been waiting for the other shoe to drop, though I was hoping maybe it wouldn't.

When I entered Dr. Butler's corner office, he was seated behind his massive desk, clearly compensating for his diminutive size. Yep, I'd thought it, and no, I wasn't sorry.

"Dr. Bruno, please take a seat," he said, gesturing to the single visitor's chair in front of the massive mahogany monstrosity. I dutifully took a seat. He sat too, his head barely clearing the top of the mammoth desk. I bit the inside of my lip to keep from smiling or laughing and looked down at my lap for a second to compose myself. I needed to get it together and act like the professional, and adult, I was.

"I have completed a cursory review of the content of the novels you publish under the pen name R.W. Cook. While Dr.

DeAngelo seems to find there to be quality content in the work, I do not necessarily agree. I find these types of foolish fantasies to be below the type of writing in which I want professors in my department to be engaged. We are an academic institution and must hold ourselves to a higher standard. Escapist fiction drawing on superhero lore is not the caliber I expect of professors in this department, especially given some of the racier themes evident in your… novels," he said, leaning forward and placing his hands on his blotter. Who even had a blotter anymore? Sheesh.

"I understand, Dr. Butler, but I do not widely promote my connection to the university in association with my pen name. I have been writing for longer than I have been a professor here, and until Dr. DeAngelo specifically mentioned my writing outside of university-sponsored publications, you were unaware of my pen name," I said, unwilling to go down without at least a little bit of a fight. Besides, as a professor of medieval literature, this man wouldn't know fantasy if it knocked him on his tiny ass.

"That is true, but as we review your application for a tenure track position, this kind of thing will factor in heavily."

"Ah, I see. Are you saying writing as R.W. Cook will count against me? Interesting, as I would assume having a published fiction author on your faculty would be a coup for you." *Take that, you old vulture.*

Dr. Butler sputtered and then narrowed his beady eyes at me. "You will need to disclose these… *works* as part of your curriculum vitae, and they will be subject to review by the entire committee. I'm uncertain whether other members of the committee will find value in these works or the messages they send about our faculty. Many are not as liberal as I am." I held back my scoff. If Armin Butler was liberal, I was Mickey Mouse.

He looked down and smoothed his hands over the blotter again before looking at me and continuing. "If you plan to continue writing these…novels, you should reassess your desire to stay at this university, Dr. Bruno. You will not be able to rely on my decades-long friendship with your father to get you past the next hurdle where the committee is concerned. In my opinion, you are too young and inexperienced to be considered for tenure, but your academic lineage and my ability to leverage my relationship with Anthony brought your name into the running. It would be a shame to disregard this opportunity over *genre fiction*." He spat the last words like they tasted foul on his tongue.

Blinking slowly, I stared at him for a moment. I wasn't sure he'd meant to disclose what he had about pulling strings to get me considered for the open spot, but instead of making me want to fight for it, I now more than ever didn't want it.

He rotated in his chair like an evil mastermind. "You are dismissed."

Not wanting to remain in the dragon's lair a moment longer, I stood and hightailed it out of there. Gah. It was asshole elitists like him and my father that made life in academia intolerable. Dr. Butler barely found value in the contemporary American literature courses I taught, and I knew several colleagues had struggled to get courses that focused on any sort of diversity approved recently. The problem wasn't me; the problem was Butler, my father, and their ilk. Unfortunately, the tenure committee had very few progressive thinkers, which meant I would have to take Dr. Butler's threat seriously. I would have to examine my desire to stay at the university and continue teaching.

I didn't love being a professor, but I did love writing. Maybe it was finally time to stop doing the easy thing. Maybe it was time to invest in my writing career full time.

Maybe it was time to do something I really wanted for a change.

14

HENRY

I KNEW something was up the second Brooks walked through the door of Tiny Tales. He looked like he'd been put through the wringer. Shoulders slumped, head down, even the bright red scarf he had wrapped around his neck looked dull.

"Babe, what's wrong?" I asked wrapping him in a hug.

"You know how I told you one of my colleagues was at the reading last week and she told the department chair? Well, he called me into his office and told me to 'reassess my desire to stay at the university' today. Apparently, the only reason I'm even being considered for tenure is because he's friends with my dad." Brooks sighed heavily as he stripped off his coat and threw it over one of the chairs in the front room near my desk.

"What does that even mean?" I asked, unsure about the implications for Brooks's future.

"I'm not really sure, but I can only imagine it means issues with my tenure track application."

Brooks and I had talked about his job and the fact he often didn't really love teaching. He saw tenure as this thing he had to achieve to make pursuing his doctorate worthwhile and to make his dad proud.

"But you're not sure you want to teach," I said, trying to get a better read on the situation so I didn't accidentally make things worse. "And you pretty much told your dad to fuck off."

"I know, but I haven't been able to write lately either. I need to get in the groove with one of my careers or else I'm not going to be doing anything." Brooks ran a hand through his hair in exasperation. "Dammit."

I had just put the finishing touches on Brooks's writing space earlier that day. I had been planning to wait until next week to show it to him, but it seemed like today might be the better time.

"Come with me," I said, grabbing his hand and pulling him toward the back of the shop where the stairs were.

"Where are we going?" he asked.

"You'll see when we get there." My heart rate had picked up, and I was almost skipping. I couldn't wait to show him the space.

"Sex chair?" he asked, his tone hopeful.

"Maybe later, but Mrs. Matthews is here, so the sex chair is currently occupied."

Brooks visibly paled and shuddered slightly. "The visual I just had on that is too much. Maybe we *should* get rid of it or move it someplace private for our use only."

I laughed. "You're the one who said, and I quote, 'Long live the sex chair.'" I pulled Brooks to the stairs and led him past the second-floor landing up to the third-floor door.

"What's up here? I thought this was all storage," he said.

"It was, but now it's… not." I opened the door and held it so he could step inside, my heart fluttering in anticipation. The first half of the space closest to the door was still storage, but past the storage area was a writer's paradise. The wide window seat in front of the leaded-glass window had a comfy cushion and plush pillows tucked into it. Shelves lined the right wall, and I'd already started filling them with books and knickknacks I'd snuck out of Brooks's house. A corner desk was tucked into the left corner with an ergonomic rolling desk chair and shelves above it for supplies and reference books. The cozy armchair Mrs. Matthews had insisted on sat next to the desk backed by a floor lamp. The new hardwood floors shone in the late afternoon light and were partially covered by a high-pile area rug in front of the chair. My favorite thing, though, was a stylized cover of *The Great Gatsby* I'd bought online and hung on the wall.

I glanced at Brooks and saw his mouth hanging open. "Do you like it?" I asked.

"This is for me?" He was staring at the space, his eyes wide and shining slightly.

"Yes. This is your Christmas present. I always thought it needed a writer to fill the space, and I've been working on it for months. When I saw your office at the apartment that night and you said you weren't feeling inspired there anymore, I knew I had to make this space yours. I want you to have a place in my shop and in my life."

"I love it." He grabbed my hand and pulled me into him, then grabbed my face with both hands and kissed me. "Now Mrs. Matthews and I can both be your shop cats."

Laughter bubbled up from my chest. "I love taking in strays." He kissed me again, and I was a little dizzy when we came up for air a few minutes later.

"I love you," Brooks whispered against my lips and then he froze and pulled back when he realized what had slipped out.

"I love you too. And I would love to have you here full time as the writer slash shop cat in my attic or part time if you stay at the university. Any way I get to be with you makes me happy."

"Me too." Brooks kissed me again and then stiffened in my arms, his face alight with a glow I'd never seen before. "Hey, is there any paper up here? I just got a great idea for a story." He turned toward the desk and found it fully stocked with notebooks, pens, and pencils. He grabbed a notebook and a pencil and flopped into the desk chair, scribbling furiously.

I sat in the armchair, which I hoped would become our new sex chair, and watched him work, grateful a southbound red line train, meddling friends, and a little good luck had brought us together.

A few minutes later, Mrs. Matthews bellowed from downstairs, and I kissed Brooks on the cheek and snuck out to see what was going on.

I found Mrs. Matthews at the bottom of the stairs, waiting with her hands on her hips and kicking the bottom stair with the toe of her leopard-print Converse sneaker.

"I see how it is. I'm good enough to exploit for manual labor, but I'm not good enough to be there for the big reveal," she said with a completely pathetic pout.

"It was sort of a spur-of-the-moment thing. You know I was planning to show him next week."

She harrumphed and turned to head back toward her spot. I had no choice but to follow.

"So, did he like it?" Mrs. Matthews asked when we'd arrived at her chair.

I couldn't stop the smile that split my face when I looked at her in the chair. It was really going to be a problem. Brooks might be onto something about hiding it somewhere more private and getting her a new one. I'd have to start checking out the resale sites.

"Judging by the look on your face, I'd say yes," she said, prodding me.

"What? Oh! Yes. He loved it. He's up there writing right now."

"Good. That's how it should be," she said, settling back into her chair.

I went to my desk by the door and sat down behind my computer. Snow was beginning to fall, and as I opened my inventory software, I thought about how completely content I felt. My man was upstairs writing. One of the other people I loved most in the world was tucked into her chair in the romance section. And I was happy.

Everything was exactly how it should be.

I had my epic romance, and Brooks was my happily ever after.

EPILOGUE
BROOKS

JANUARY – ONE YEAR LATER

ONCE AGAIN TINY TALES was packed, and Stacey and I were squished into a corner in the romance room as we waited for people to settle so she could introduce me before I read from my latest novel and then did an intimate signing. Unlike the first signing I'd done at the shop, this was the exclusive launch party for my newest book and a ticketed event. The tickets had gone fast since there were so few available, given the size of the venue. All fifty had sold on the first day.

"I'm really glad you decided to do this," Stacey said, looking out over the crowd that was still mostly milling around the shop.

"What? This party?" I asked.

She scoffed. It was the sound I associated with moments when she thought I was being an idiot. "No. Writing full time. I think this year has been really good for you. You seem happier than I've seen you in a long time."

I caught Henry's eye from across the room through the arched doorway, and he gave me a small wave before returning his focus to the customer in front of him. "Yeah. I agree. Academia wasn't for me. This is much better." Shortly after Dr. Butler's not-so-veiled ultimatum, I withdrew my tenure application, and after I submitted my final grades for the fall semester, I started writing full time. Henry and I had talked a lot about the decision, and he'd been my biggest champion since I'd left teaching.

My father hadn't been pleased, but his annoyance had more to do with his ego and looking bad in front of a friend than it had to do with my decision to abandon life as a professor. Henry had sent him a copy of the review and the ranking list when my first novel after leaving academia hit number two on the *USA Today* bestsellers list. He'd called and left a perfunctory message of congratulations that ended with a barb about how number two wasn't number one. I hadn't called him back. Henry was holding out hope he'd come around. I didn't much care either way. We'd never been all that close, and the family I'd formed with Henry and Mrs. Matthews was everything I needed at the moment.

I'd put out seven new books since, most part of a queer contemporary romantic suspense and thriller series where the main characters meet through chance encounters and are forced into impossible situations orchestrated by a mysterious criminal mastermind. It was my own experiment in art—loosely—imitating life, and to hear Stacey tell it, it was paying off. I had attracted a ton of new readers, and because of the bump in reader-ship, Stacey and Henry had ganged up on me and made me attend my first national signing.

Looking back now, I really couldn't complain about the long weekend spent in Portland, Oregon, with Henry. The event had been well organized, and Henry had acted as my personal assistant. The hotel sex had been exuberant and acrobatic and made our time spent on the sex chair, which still lived in the romance room, look tame.

We had both met Janet Evanovich and gotten one of her books signed for Mrs. Matthews. Since then Mrs. Matthews had stopped questioning my legitimacy as an author, but she had started dropping hints that she'd like to go with us to the next event. Neither of us were trying to encourage that idea.

"I know that look," Stacey said, returning my attention to the event at hand. "Please don't tell me what you're thinking about. I don't want to know." I laughed, and she fluffed her short dark hair, straightened her red suit jacket, and checked her watch before turning to me. "It's almost showtime. Are you ready?"

I rolled my shoulders and took a deep breath, taking in the lemon, paper, and ink smell of the shop I loved. I wrote there full time now, tucked away in my upstairs nook, and after I'd gone cliché and given Henry a key to my apartment for Christmas last year, we'd been coming to the shop every morning together. A hint of Henry's citrusy cologne swirled in the air. It was a scent I associated with home, and it settled any nerves I had. "Ready as I'll ever be," I said, shooting Stacey a smile.

She placed a hand on my arm and looked at me seriously. "And what about for the other thing?"

I patted my suit coat pocket and felt the small box there. "So ready."

She smiled and went up on her tiptoes to kiss my cheek. "I can't wait. Let's get this party started." With a quick wink over her shoulder, she called the room to order and asked everyone to take their seats. She ran through a brief introduction, and I took my place in the sex chair as was tradition.

As I started to read, I glanced out over the assembled crowd. Henry was leaning in the arched doorway, and he blew me a small kiss. My heart turned over in my chest. I had never known love like I had with him. I was so lucky to have him in my life, and I still couldn't believe a random encounter on the train had brought us together. Our story had been the inspiration for my newest series, and that had made Henry swoon when he read the first few chapters of the first book. But now I was ready to start our next chapter.

I finished the passage I had selected and turned to the front of the book, flipping it face down on the table next to the chair to hold the place. I looked up at Henry and motioned him forward.

"Before I open the floor for questions, I have something else I'd like to read." I had kept the dedication for this final book in the series a secret, and I wanted to share it with Henry as a surprise.

Henry had made his way farther into the room, but he was hiding in a corner by Stacey. I walked over and took his hand, dragging him to the front of the crowd.

"As some of you know, this is Henry Miller. He is the owner of Tiny Tales and our gracious host this evening." Henry blushed as the crowd applauded politely. My heart was beating double time, and I dropped Henry's hand so I could surreptitiously wipe my now damp palms on my pants. Big public displays weren't my thing, but they were Henry's, and this was about to be his moment. I didn't want him to know I was nervous.

"What you may not know is that Henry is my partner, and parts of our story—obviously not the murders or heists—inspired my Forced Connections series. Without Henry, this series wouldn't have happened, and I'd like to share something with all of you." I picked up the book and read.

"For my dearest Hopeless Romantic. Who would have thought my own stranger on the train would turn out to be my soul mate. The love you have brought into my life has brought me immeasurable joy, inspired me in boundless ways, and sparked many questions, but none as important as…" I set down the book, sank to one knee, and pulled out the ring box I'd had made to look like a tiny version of *Kryptonite*. I took Henry's hand and looked into his gorgeous face. His green eyes were sparkling with tears behind his perfectly nerdy glasses.

"Henry Miller, will you marry me?" I asked, popping the ring box open with one hand to reveal a simple band.

Henry was sobbing in earnest now but nodding frantically. I stood and wrapped him in my arms, and he whispered, "Yes, yes, a thousand times yes," into my ear. I pulled back and kissed him, and the room erupted into cheers and catcalls.

Stacey opened a bottle of champagne, and plastic champagne flutes appeared seemingly out of nowhere. We each took a flute and sipped as bottles of bubbly circulated around the room and we accepted congratulations and well-wishes from the attendees.

Shortly after, I settled myself behind the table set up for the signing and got to work. Many people wanted me to date the books since this date was now significant to me, and I was happy to oblige. By the time the last book was signed and the last person left, I was exhausted and my face hurt from smiling. Stacey had been busy tidying up and taking down chairs for the last half hour, so there wasn't much left for Henry and me to do.

I tossed my pen down onto the table as Henry went to lock the door and pull the shade.

"Another successful event in the books, Brooks!" Stacey said with a giggle. "Books... Brooks. That rhymes!" She giggled again, and I rolled my eyes.

"Exactly how much champagne did you have, Stace?" Henry asked, looking at her over his glasses in a move very reminiscent of Mrs. Matthews.

"I lost track after the fourth glass. It was still less than her." Stacey gestured over her shoulder into the romance room where Mrs. Matthews was passed out in the sex chair with her feet propped up on her giant turquoise bag.

We all burst into laughter, and Mrs. Matthews stirred in the chair then resettled with a snort and snore.

"I'll go wake her up, and we'll get out of your hair," Stacey said, heading off to rouse her.

Henry turned and pulled me up out of my chair, and I wrapped my arms around his neck. "I love you, Brooks," he whispered into my neck.

"I love you too," I said, nipping his ear and moving to kiss his jaw.

"Enough canoodling. We'll be out of here in a minute," Mrs. Matthews said, shuffling into the room with Stacey right behind her carrying the turquoise beast. We broke apart and each gave Mrs. Matthews a hug. Her eyes were a little unfocused, and her gray-and-white hair was sticking up in all directions on one side of her head while the other side was completely flat. "I do love you boys, though. And congratulations again." She patted Henry's cheek fondly then turned toward the door, fumbling with the lock and muttering to herself about "shoddy craftsmanship."

"I love you guys too," Stacey said. "I ordered us an Uber, and I'll make sure she gets home. Let's grab brunch tomorrow before I head back to New York."

"Sounds good," I said as Stacey hugged me. "You pick the place and time, and we'll be there."

"Good." Stacey hugged Henry and gave him a quick kiss on the cheek, then followed Mrs. Matthews out. Henry locked the door behind them and dimmed the lights, and we watched the ladies get into a car and drive away.

I wrapped Henry in my arms from behind and he held his left hand up, admiring the tungsten band on his ring finger. I had wanted something as indestructible as the love I felt for him.

"Have you read the inscription yet?" I asked.

"There's an inscription?"

"There is. Read it." Henry slipped the ring off and held it up to the dim light. A vein of bright green malachite ran along the inside, and he gasped as he turned the ring and saw the words I'd had etched there.

"You are my kryptonite," Henry read before slipping the ring back on and sliding his hands around my neck.

"Seemed appropriate. I love you so much, sometimes it feels like I'm going to combust. You are my greatest weakness, but your love is my greatest strength." A single happy tear slid down his cheek and I kissed it away. "I can't wait to write the rest of our story."

"Neither can I."

THE END

***

Want more Open Doors? Check out the rest of the series here:
https://mybook.to/OpenDoorsSeries

Check out all the Open Doors bonus content here:
https://www.prolificworks.com/author/vinnigeorge

ALSO BY VINNI GEORGE

The Open Doors Series

Hold the Door

Door Number Two

Revolving Door

Doors Open on the Left

A Foot in the Door

The Hidden Door

Standalone Shorts

Story Hour

Shifter MPREG

Jonah and the Narwhal

Everett and the Wolf (Coming 2023!)

ABOUT THE AUTHOR

Vinni George has been a lover of romance novels (of all shapes, sizes, and colors) since she first got her hands on one of her grandmother's Harlequins and has never looked back. She lives in Ohio with her two favorite guys (her husband and son) and, hopefully—one day—a dog. When not writing her own stories, she can be found helping to polish other people's novels. In her spare time, Vinni dabbles in performance art, quilting, and various culinary pursuits and enjoys traveling.

Vinni's debut novel, *Hold the Door*, was a finalist and runner-up in Contemporary Gay Romance in the 2020-2021 Rainbow Awards.

Connect with Vinni:
Sign up for Vinni's newsletter at vinnigeorge.com.
Join Vinni's Facebook reader group George's Jungle.

facebook.com/vinni-george-3

instagram.com/vinnigeorgewrites

goodreads.com/Vinni_George

amazon.com/Vinni-George/e/B0912X5MNL/ref=aufs_dp_fta_dsk

bookbub.com/profile/vinni-george

www.ingramcontent.com/pod-product-compliance
Lightning Source LLC
Chambersburg PA
CBHW021010160726

47994CB00006B/2458